A SHOOTER'S AMBITION 2

S. Allen

Lock Down Publications and Ca$h
Presents
A Shooter's Ambition 2
A Novel by _S. Allen_

S. Allen

Lock Down Publications
P.O. Box 870494
Mesquite, Tx 75187

Copyright 2020 by S. Allen
A Shooter's Ambition 2

Lock Down Publications
Like our page on Facebook: Lock Down Publications @
www.facebook.com/lockdownpublications.ldp
Cover design and layout by: **Dynasty Cover Me**
Book interior design by: **Shawn Walker**
Edited by: **Sunny Giovani**

Stay Connected with Us!

Text **LOCKDOWN** to 22828 to stay up-to-date with new releases, sneak peaks, contests and more…

Thank you!

Submission Guideline.

Submit the first three chapters of your completed manuscript to ldpsubmissions@gmail.com, subject line: Your book's title. The manuscript must be in a .doc file and sent as an attachment. Document should be in Times New Roman, double spaced and in size 12 font. Also, provide your synopsis and full contact information. If sending multiple submissions, they must each be in a separate email.

Have a story but no way to send it electronically? You can still submit to LDP/Ca$h Presents. Send in the first three chapters, written or typed, of your completed manuscript to:

LDP: Submissions Dept
P.O. Box 870494
Mesquite, Tx 75187

DO NOT send original manuscript. Must be a duplicate.

Provide your synopsis and a cover letter containing your full contact information.

Thanks for considering LDP and Ca$h Presents.

Dedication

This book is dedicated to my loving mother Karen Collins. Words cannot express how much I love you. Just know that your dreams of us walking down the beach in Florida is not a dream but will very soon become a reality. I also dedicate this book to my cousin Tamara Dunnkin. RIP. You were so smart, sweet and kind. Even at our very young age you showed me the importance of education as you always had a book in your hands. I know it is you that protects and looks over me from the heavens above. I hope that I make you proud, my angel.

Acknowledgements

Shoutout to CA$H and my LDP family for giving me a shot to do what I do with this pen. Special shout out to all my fans and those that support the S. Allen movement. I appreciate all the love. You are the ones that motivate me to keep dropping this gangsta shit! And trust and believe I will never let you down.

S. Allen

S. Allen

Prologue

"On today's stop story, the Chicago police have released the name of a murder suspect, suspected to have been involved in at least five homicides. Let's go to Dionte Collins who is live at the scene at the Kedzie and Harrison Street Precinct. Dionte, can you tell us what's going on in the case of Byron Hobson? Is he charged with the murders?"

"From what we know, Byron Hobson has been sought by Chicago police for five homicides. Standing right here with us is the Chief of Police. Chief, can you tell us what's going on in this case?"

"Byron Hobson is in question. He is ex-military, has extreme sniper training, and has been named to the best sniper the United States of America has produced. We have evidence that says these shootings were executed with someone who has official accuracy or rifle training. Mr. Hobson is considered to be armed and dangerous, and we'd like anybody who knows the whereabouts of Byron Hobson to contact the police immediately."

"Alright, thanks, Chief."

"No problem."

"And you have heard it right here from Chicago's Chief of Police. If you see Byron Hobson, contact police immediately or crime stoppers, at 626-0693. Back to you, Vanessa."

"You see that shit?" Killa Fred said turning down the volume on the 70-inch plasma TV that was mounted on the wall.

Mr. Biggs and his goons were at a building on 15th and Kedzie, one of their strong holds on the city's Westside. They were about to take over the Mafia's block on Averas and Agusta. Mr. Biggs scheduled a meeting with the rest of the membership at a warehouse on 95th and Jeffery. If they were to come at Byron and the Mafia's, they had to come hard as the news had revealed that their enemy was not the average Joe but a cold-blooded assassin. It was time to get active and Mr. Biggs needed all his men on point and ready for war.

"Yea, I see it, but I don't. This nigga definitely been cruising for a bruising. That's why we gotta find him and kill 'em." Mr. Biggs replied.

"I think he just on a suicide mission. We gone show 'em he faking with this murder shit." Body Bag said, putting a 30-round clip magazine in a MPS machine gun. At the same time Killa Fred was pulling a Kevlar Vest over his chest.

"After tonight I want this shit done and over with; you understand?" Mr. Biggs said checking the clip to his 911 .45.

Mr. Biggs and his henchmen continued loading their weapons, getting ready to bring the drama to Byron and the Mafia's. Tonight, they were going to rush Averas and Agusta with all the soldiers and pistols they had. In the end, Mr. Biggs would have taken over a $100,000 a night heroin block. The money was his motivation, and he was willing to put his life on the line to obtain it. Mr. Biggs and his men left the building on their way to 95th and Jeffery to meet up with the rest of his army, and then to Averas and Agusta to eliminate his enemies.

***

Byron sat in his black T-top '87 Monte Carlos SS. He was in a murderous mind state parked across the street in front of the 1514 building on Kedzie Avenue. His palms sweaty as he gripped the Mac-90 that rested on his lap. Now was the moment of truth; it was either kill or be killed, and Byron wasn't in the mood for dying.

Byron counted four of Mr. Biggs security standing in front of the building. His initial plan was to run up kamikaze style, but the activity in front of the building looked as if Mr. Biggs would come out soon, so he patiently waited. Sunk low in the seat of the SS, Byron watched the front of the building. He could see that the individuals in front of the building were armed. Byron's patience paid off as he noticed Mr. Biggs and three more men exit the building. After calmly pulling down his black ski-mask, he pulled the slide of the Mac-90, injecting a round into the chamber and then stepped out the whip.

Cha-cha-cha-cha-cha! Byron squeezed the trigger, lighting up the dark street. A few of The Body Snatchers returned fire. Byron ducked behind the SS and applied relentless pressure to the trigger.

Cha-cha-cha-cha-cha-cha! Hot shell casings covered the pavement as Byron continued to fire. Killa Fred pulled Mr. Biggs down behind a parked car to shield him from the assault of the 7.62 rounds being sent in their direction.

Body Bag sprayed led from the MPS, which made Byron get low but continuing to fire, hitting one of the bodyguards in the face, leaving him sprawled out on the concrete. Byron focused his aim on Mr. Biggs who was pinned down behind a car. *Cha-cha-cha-cha!* The loud rifle barked and jerked in Byron's hand. After emptying the 30-round magazine Byron jumped back in his car. He pulled off, leaving a bloody mess. He would get at Mr Biggs's cronies another time. Getting the head, he knew the body would crumble.

"Two-two-three, we have a report of shots fired on Fifteenth and Kedzie. I repeat, Two-two-three, we have a report of shots fired on Fifteenth and Kedzie." The dispatcher said over the radio.

Detective Calhoun was in the McDonald's on Kedzie and Roosevelt, getting a cup of coffee when the call came over the radio. "Got-dammit." He cursed as he raced out of the McDonald's parking lot. He was only a few blocks away from the shooting as he gunned his Crown Victoria down Kedzie. Detective Calhoun put the police light on top of the hood and activated it. He had a feeling that Byron had something to do with the shooting. He wanted nothing more in life than to deliver Byron personally to the Menard Penitentiary with a fresh 100-year sentence. Detective Calhoun saw a shiny black Monte Carlos speeding toward his way on the other side of Kedzie. When the car passed him, he looked to the left and got a view of the driver. He couldn't believe his eyes as he slammed on the brakes, bringing his car to a screeching halt before he made a U-turn in pursuit of the SS.

Byron had just crossed the bridge on Kedzie and Roosevelt when he looked in his rearview mirror and saw the Crown Victoria with the sirens blaring. "Fuck!" Byron cursed as he slowed his car down at a traffic light on Kedzie and Madison. He was in a jam as he was behind 3 cars. The police car pulled beside Byron, and once Byron saw the pale-faced cracker Detective Calhoun screaming for him to pull over he knew he had to make a move. Turning the wheel to the right Byron pulled carefully out of the box he was in and stomped on the gas pedal, shooting the car across the intersection on Kedzie and Madison like a rocket.

Looking in his rearview he saw that Calhoun was still in hot pursuit. Byron's main objective was to ditch the cop and make it back to Averas and Agusta. A stinging sensation on the side of his stomach caused him to feel it. What he felt was wetness, and after examining his hand he knew now that he had been shot.

Byron raced down Kedzie Street as the 600 horsepower under the hood had him leaving the Crown Victoria in the dust. Byron made a quick right on Franklin Street and smashed the gas. The Magnaflow pipes howled as he made a left on Trey. Looking in the rearview, the Crown Victoria was nowhere in sight. At that moment Byron was glad he invested the $9,000 on the Monte Carlos, as the car was made for sticky situations, and eluding Detective Calhoun was definitely a sticky situation.

Byron grabbed his cellphone and dialed a number. He had been reluctant to use the number but now he had no choice. The phone rang as Byron glided down Chicago Avenue. He was only a few blocks from his home, then the person on the other line answered.

"Hello."

"Sergeant Hobson, how's it going?"

"You still calling me Sergeant, huh?" Byron said with a slight chuckle, the pain in his stomach becoming unbearable. "Listen, I need a favor. You told me to call if I ever needed one, and Commander Sanchez, I really need one."

"Anything, Hobson," Commander Sanchez replied.

Byron proceeded to tell him what he needed, until he pulled in front of his home. After giving Byron his word he would take care of it, Byron grabbed his Mac-90, got out the SS and painfully walked inside his home.

"I need all units to the block of ten-forty-eight North Averas. I repeat, all units to the block of ten-forty-eight North Averas." Detective Calhoun said over the radio. He was pissed that he had lost Byron, but his Crown Victoria was no match for the Monte Carlos.

Detective Calhoun knew Byron was on the way to Averas and Agusta. Tonight, Byron was going either of two places. To jail or the morgue, and Detective Calhoun was adamant about being the one to send him to either of the two. He was headed to Averas and Agusta to confront one of Chicago's most wanted.

Byron sat in his mother's home loading a 100-round drum for the Mac-90. The pain from his gunshot wound was excruciating. He took a swig from a bottle of Bacardi 131 that Lil' Pooh left, to ease the pain. He was in war mode as he was on a mission. A mission to kill. He was riding for his mother, for Juice, for Lil' Pooh, for Noody, for Carmella, Billy Good and Rico, and the Mafia's organization as a whole. After loading the last shell into the drum, he stuck it under the rifle, locked it and loaded it.

"Byron Hobson, this is the Chicago Police Department! We have your home surrounded! Come out with your hands up! I repeat, come out with your hands up!"

Byron got up and peeked out the curtain, seeing what looked to be at least 5 squad cars on the block with officers standing with AR-15's and shotguns pointed at his house. He knew he had a decision to make. Everything he had loved was gone, he had nobody; it was him against the world. Byron hit the liquor one more time before he stuck the Mac-90 out the window. And fired.

S. Allen

Chapter 1

Cha-Cha! The roar from M1-Carbine could be heard from far out. The shooter firing the weapon missed the bullseye by two inches. "Malaki. I told you breathe. Relax. Squeeze." Commander Sanchez said to 18-year-old Malaki, who was his oldest and only son.

18 years earlier Commander Sanchez was sitting in his home in South Dakota when he received a late-night phone call from an old friend. The friend was stressed. The two men had become good friends in the military and had been through many trials and tribulations together. His friend was a lethal sniper for the military and would have given his life to the United States of America and its political. His friend was in a life and death situation and it was no way he could turn his back on him. Commander Sanchez went to the Department of Children Family Services and passed as Byron's brothers. The intent at the time didn't have a name, a family, or home. But by Byron giving his life to the United States he would make sure the child would have a future. He owed Byron that much. Commander Sanchez was a first-time father so everything about fatherhood he learned on a day to day basis. He named the boy Malaki, and over the years he had grown to love Byron's seed.

Commander Sanchez performed his investigation and feuded beyond criminal activities. The murders committed by the former Marine, and him being involved with gang leadership. Commander Sanchez was disappointed in what Bryon got involved in it, but in his eyes, Bryon was still the best damn sniper the United State had ever produced.

When young Malaki was at the tender age of 13, Commander had given him the real story about his mother and father and how they were brutally murdered in the cold streets of Chicago. It was at the moment Malaki wanted to see revenge on his parents' murders. Young Malaki was set on revenge and wanted nothing more. Commander Sanchez kept Malaki out of the eye of the public. He was homeschooled in academies. Commander Sanchez made sure he worked out relentlessly, and because of his 6'1" frame he was chiseled with plenty of definition. His skin was a light caramel complexion like his mother but he had his father's heart and ambition.

When Malaki became of age, he was trained in firearms as well as explosives. He mastered all rifles manufactured to men with the .50 caliber being his favorite. Malaki was also a third-degree black belt and was a beast at hand-to-hand combat.

Malaki sat the M-1 Carbine down. "Papa, I am relaxing. I don't like the Carbine." Malaki stated as he stood up and dusted off his fatigue cargo pants. "And plus, I'm tired. I have been shooting all day." It was only 12:00 in the afternoon and he had already shot 2,000 rounds from different weapons.

Commander Sanchez took a pull from his Cuban Cigar before he spoke. "My son, you have to be qualified with all the weapons." Commander Sanchez put his chubby hand on Malaki's shoulder.

"Yes, Papa." Malaki nodded.

"Well, my son. Always know that in the battlefield your enemies will not care if you are tired. They will proceed to do everything in their power to end your life. Do you understand?"

"I understand, papa." Malaki responded in understanding.

"Good, because in due time it will be time. Time to go to Chicago and loyalty avenge your parents' blood that was shed."

At the mention of his deceased parents, Malaki was given a dose of morale. He had wasted and trained his entire life to seize that moment and he would not let it slip through his grasp. Malaki picked up the American-made weapon, ejected the 30-round magazine and inserted a new one. Laying in his stomach he zeroed in on the target with the OP 360 long-range scope. He was 2,500 meters away. Sliding the shot back, a 7.62 round was ready to be released from the barrel. Malaki took a short breath, relaxing with his finger resting on the trigger. After a slow and steady squeeze the rifle kicked into his right shoulder. After the Carbine came into sight, Malaki saw that he hit the bullseye and was right back on target as he let the rifle back two more times, both slugs penetrating the bullseye.

Commander Sanchez pulled out is binoculars to view the marksmanship. A smile plastered his face. Malaki stood up leaving the smoking rifle on the ground before he walked over to his father.

Without looking at his son, Commander Sanchez lowered the binoculars and said, "Son, that was good shooting, but I want you to continue to practice your trade. Remember, practice makes perfect."

"Yes, papa."

"Now, go and rest. Tomorrow we do more shooting." Commander wanted Malaki to be the best in his trade, and once in Chicago, it would be dealing death.

S. Allen

Chapter 2

Killa Fred stepped from the Bentley GT Coup that sat on 26-inch Giovanna rims. The dope game had been good to him working as Mr. Biggs' henchman and second command. After the death of Byron, Mr. Biggs and the Body Snatchers continued their business venture with the Mexican Cartel boss Castilino, and in time began to plan his demise. The murder of Castilino, leader of the Madina Cartel, failed at the hands of the Body Snatchers. Even in failure, the gang managed to get away with 1,000 kilos of uncut heroin. In time the Body Snatchers climbed to the top of the drug trade, reigning supreme. All that opposed them or went against the laws of the land were laid down by Mr. Biggs and his faculty. Mr. Biggs was head honcho in the city of the Chi and the Midwest as a whole, flooding the streets of Minnesota, Cleveland, Indiana and other major cities with dope. Killa Fred hit the alarm on the Bentley and headed into Ryan's Steakhouse where he was to attend a meeting with Mr. Biggs and his protege Body Bags. There was a problem within the organization that had to be dealt with pertaining to a shortage in profit coming from Minnesota.

Walking through the crowded restaurant Killa Fred glanced at his diamond studded Frank Mueller watch. He has a few minutes early but smiled when he saw Mr. Biggs and Body Bag seated at a table in the back of the restaurant.

"What's good fam? Took you long enough." Mr. Biggs greeted with a smirk. Extending his hand, his $50,000 pinky ring shined when the light hit it.

Killa Fred joked and took a seat at the table.

"What's good, Killa?" Body Bag greeted after downing his double shot of Patron. Killa Fred nodded at the young goon before him.

An Italian, curvaceous waiter approached the men at the table to take their orders. "Excuse me, gentlemen, are you ready to order?" She asked with a seductive look in her eyes.

"Give us a few minutes, lil' mama." Body Bag retorted, eyeing her thick thighs.

The waitress caught the look and replied in a sexy voice, "Alright. When you're ready, just let me know," and walked off with an extra switch in her hips knowing that all eyes were on her ass.

"Damn, I might have to run up in that."

"You run up in everything. That's your problem now." Killa talked.

"Call it what you want, but shorty like that."

"Now check this out," Mr. Biggs intervened getting to business. "This nigga Peter Gunz out in Minnesota seem to have a lil' problem on how he's conducting his business and we're having a lil' misunderstanding about some money he owe me."

Killa Fred's eyebrow raised in interest. "What kind of misunderstanding?"

"The nigga say the last 20-brick shipment wasn't the same demonstation we have been giving him. Says he lost out big on the work." Mr. Biggs explained.

"That's game fam. All the shit the same— same weight, same stamp, same cut. That nigga horse playing."

"I know that and you know that. We have been giving him bricks for a while now and it's funny how he now wants to play games."

"So what he talking about now?" Body Bag asked.

"This cat owe 1.2-mill off the shipment… Now he is saying since he took a loss, he only coming with half the money."

Both Body Bag and Killa Fred erupted in laughter.

"That's how I feel." Mr. Biggs said with an evil smirk.

"When you want us to go holler at this clown?" Body Bag asked ready to lay his murder game down.

Mr. Biggs' smirk turned sinister and serious. "Fuck the money. I want his life. It ain't about the money no more, it's about his disrespect."

Killa Fred nodded his head in understanding. Money would come and go but respect and fear must always be ingrained in the men you deal with. "Say no more, Boss Man. Considered that shit done."

"I'm just curious. Who dropped the birds in Minnesota anyway?" Mr. Biggs asked.

"I had Lil' Tony and Ronnie handle that function." Killa Fred replied.

"Do you trust them?"

"Yeah. Them my lil' men. They have been with us for a few years now. They always handle the business and they are always on point."

"Alright. Just make sure shit is handled properly on our end and keep your eyes open, but I want this Gunz issue dealt with ASAP within the next 48 hours." Mr. Biggs ordered.

Body Bag stood up from the table and straightened his pants leg.

"Where are you going? You are not going to eat?" Killa Fred asked.

"Naw, I gotta bounce. I gotta go check on something."

"Well, we might as well leave at the same time." Mr. Biggs said.

The three killers exited the restaurant. Standing in front of Ryan's Steakhouse the men shook hands and went their own ways. It was plenty of money and plenty of blood to be spilled.

Across the street a man sat low in the seat of a rented Dodge Challenger. Watching the men through his binoculars he had a decision to make. He could easily hop out and spray them down with the Bushmaster 223 assault rifle that laid on his passenger seat next to him. It was broad daylight in downtown Chicago. As soon as gunshots rang, the police would have him boxed in, so that wasn't an option. And knowing the man's aim, shit could get real ugly, real quick. So, he figured he would just continue with his surveillance on his enemies, and when time presented itself, he would step up and crush all in involved.

***

"Ooooh, Papi, don't stop... Don't stop." The petite Latina screamed while Peter Gunz banged her pussy up from the back.

The fat ass and small waist had him in a trance as he watched his nine-inch pole slide in and out of Maria's tight walls. "Damn, bitch, I'm about to bust." Peter Gunz grabbed a fist full of her shoulder-length hair.

"No, baby, not yet." Her pleas for stamina fell on deaf ears as he released his seeds into her warmth and wetness.

"Damn, girl." Peter Gunz continued to pump into her until all of his kids were in her. Laying on his back, spent from the sex, sweat covered his body.

"Damn, Papi," Marcia said planting kisses on his heaving chest all while gripping and jerking his deflating dick, trying to get it back hard.

Peter Gunz was a Puerto Rican who ran the streets of St. Paul, Minnesota. After being released from Feds for a drug conspiracy he hit the streets full throttle, getting back to the money. Being in love with cars, clothes and hoes he retreated back to the only thing he knew. The dope game. He met Mr. Biggs at a Don-Diva event in Baltimore some years back, and it was at that time Mr. Biggs fronted him his first brick of heroin. It didn't take Peter Gunz that long to climb to the top of the drug trade, after recruiting a vicious squad of killers to enhance and protect his empire. The money came along with the thirst for power, along with the cockiness. Peter Gunz rested his head in a lavish mansion overlooking the twin cities of Minnesota. A Bentley Ghost, a Maserati and a green Lamborghini Harran rested in the circular driveway of his crib. His lavish lifestyle cost millions, that's why tried his hand with Mr. Biggs, claiming the product wasn't the same and that he took a loss, only able to give him half of the $1.2-million. He had been doing business with Mr. Biggs for a few years and brought him millions in drug money and figured he should get a play on the bricks. Mr. Biggs was giving him the bricks on consignment for $80,000 a brick, and Peter Gunz felt he should be getting them for a cheaper ticket. He was being greedy and didn't figure his greediness would lead him to his grace.

Killa Fred and Body Bag sat in an Orkin van, smoking a blunt of Purple Haze. A track from Do or Die played low in the background.

Body Bag inhaled the potent THC. "How many you think in there?"

"He got two bodyguards that I know of," Killa Fred replied.

The two murderers were dressed in Orkin exterminator uniforms. They would use the uniform to penetrate the security and get them through the front door. Light Kevlar vests rested under the uniforms while silenced Glocks where concealed on their waistlines.

"Nigga, you got 17 in that hammer plus my 17. I doubt it's 34 niggas laying around in there, and if it is, you know what it is. Murder-Murder. Kill-Kill."

Body Bag shook his head from side to side. "You never cease to amaze me. Let's just go handle this shit so we can get back to the Chi." He grabbed his Glock and cocked it.

Killa Fred put the van in drive, pulled into the circular driveway of the mansion and parked behind one of the foreign whips. "Let's get active, youngin."

The two exited the whip and made their way to the front door of the mansion. Once at the door, Killa Fred pressed the doorbell with the silenced Glock 30 hidden behind his back. Body Bag stood off to the side locked and loaded, ready for action.

After a minute the door to the mansion opened. "What the fuck you want?" A big, linebacker looking dude with cornrows asked from the other side of the door. The handle of a 45 rested in the confines of his Robin Jeans.

"Sir, we are from Orkin. We got a call saying that your residence has problem with termites." Killa Fred sounding professional.

"You must have the wrong crib. No termites in here."

Killa Fred noticed another bodyguard playing a video game on a large television. The smell of high-grade Mannequin greeted him in the doorway. He knew these men were not on point and that mistake would cost them their lives. "Alright, my brother. Must be the wrong address."

As Killa Fred turned to walk away, Body Bag stepped in front of the doorway, extended his Glock in the man's face and squeezed the trigger. *Psssst. Pssst.* Two to the head splattered the man's brains and skull fragments through the back of his melon in a pinkish mess that smelled of copper. He was dead before his body hit the floor. Killa Fred stepped over the dead corpse and turned toward the guard playing the video game. The guard heard the footsteps and was about to react to the situation. He reached for his gun a milli second too late. Killa Fred put a slug through the back of his head, plastering his brains and thoughts on the PlayStation console as Body Bag closed the front door.

"Where the fuck this clown at?"

"Papi, you gone take me shopping like you said?" Maria asked as she slid off the bed and put her hair in a ponytail.

Peter Gunz admired her body and immediately got another erection, ready for round three of wild, passionate sex. "I told you I got you, shorty. Where are you going?" Peter Gunz asked watching Maria put on her Victoria's Secret thong.

"I have to go pee."

"Well, hurry up. My anaconda waiting on you." He said stroking his manhood.

Maria smiled and walked out of the bedroom while Peter Gunz watched her ass jiggle with each step.

Killa Fred and Body Bag proceeded to the spiral staircase, headed for the second floor of the mansion with their guns extended in front of them ready to bust. Walking past a door they heard the toilet flush. Killa Fred put a finger to his lips. Body Bag knew to be quiet.

Maria got off the toilet and flushed it. She was feeling good off the Molly and the dick that Peter Gunz was slinging and was hoping to get an outfit out of the deal. After washing her hands, she stepped out of the bathroom and was greeted with automatics pointing in her face.

Peter Gunz was lost in his thoughts when Maria came through the bedroom door, a scared look on her face. "What the fuck wrong with you?" He asked sitting up in his king size bed.

Maria never got a chance to answer, her brains exploded from the front of her forehead. Her body hit the floor with a loud thud.

"What's good, Pretty Ricky? You owe Mr. Biggs some bread?" Killa Fred asked getting straight to the point. The smoking Glock still in his hand now pointing in Peter Gunz's direction.

Peter Gunz was horrified as he watched Maria's blood spill on his Persian rug. "Man, listen. I have the money. It's in the safe. Please don't shoot me."

Body Bag laughed. "What's the combination, pussy?"

"10-2-79," Peter Gunz spilled.

"See, all you had to do was give the old man his money. Now look at you." Killa Fred retorted.

"Fam, it's just a misunderstanding. I was going to get him the money." Peter Gunz pleaded.

"Well it's all good. He ain't tripping," was all Killa Fred said before he emptied his clip in Peter Gunz's body littering his bed sheets with brains and shell casings.

Body Bag continued to empty the safe, putting stacks of money into a Gucci bag he found in the closet. The two gangsters left the mansion with four more bodies added to their belts and their thirst quenched from the bloodshed.

"Hold up a minute," Body Bag said and ran back in the mansion.

S. Allen

Chapter 3

Malaki jumped up from doing his last set of pushups. He already did 1,500 earlier that day and was now finishing another 1,500. Today was strength training. Three days of the week was dedicated to his strength build up and the other days were calisthenics, and accuracy shooting with different rifles and handguns, as well as an assault weapon. Since he was born, he had been at Commander Sanchez's ranch in South Dakota. He loved Commander Sanchez like a father and was grateful for his parenting. Commander Sanchez raised Malaki to be a thoroughbred assassin.

Malaki's life took a turn in emotional turmoil when Commander Sanchez told him he was not his biological father. He told him about his mother being gunned down in the streets like a dog by Mr. Biggs' hitman as they attempted to murder his father. Malaki was told his father went out guns blazing against the Chicago Police Department. His killer… Detective Calhoun.

"Your father was a good man and loyal soldier for the United States of America." Commander Sanchez explained the missions Byron completed for Malaki and how his father awes most wanted by the Taliban and Al Qaeda groups. Malaki was intrigued by his father's tradition and history and looked up to the man he will never know as his hero. His parents were murdered in the streets of Chicago, he would never have his mother's love or nourishing. Malaki decided he would find his parents' killers and bring them the same fate that his parents were dealt if it was the last thing he did in life.

Malaki stood up and wiped the sweat from his forehead. He looked in the wall size mirror inside the gym that was built on Commander Sanchez's ranch. He admired his chiseled body. Looking at his reflection was like starting at his father. Malaki had seen plenty military pictures of his father. He knew he was Byron's son and that his blood ran deep in his veins. And that was enough to give him even more ambition to avenge his parents' murders. Malaki knew that he was read— mentally, physically and spiritually— to punish his enemies and anybody tryign to stop him. Commander Sanchez and Malaki had devised a plan to penetrate Mr. Biggs' infrastructure. He would enter the deadly dope game of the streets of Chicago, rock his enemies to sleep and eternally lay them to rest.

Commander Sanchez walked inside the gym. "My son, I thought I might find you here."

"Yes, papa, I was just finishing up my training." Malaki replied, slipping his Under Armor muscle shirt over his upper body.

"What's wrong, son? Everything alright?" Commander Sanchez questioned, noticing Malaki's distant mood.

"Papa, I'm ready." Malaki said looking into his father's eyes.

Commander Sanchez thought harder before he spoke. He knew that Malaki was well equipped with more than enough training to hunt and punish his enemies. He also knew that the deadly gangster in the violent city played for keeps when it came to homicide, and their record high of 800 bodies that year was living proof.

If Malaki entered the blood-soaked battlefield and failed, the only result would be his death and that was something he couldn't bear to lose; somebody he had grown to love wholeheartedly. It would kill him. Looking in his son's eyes he could see the ambition and pain. If he didn't let Malaki have the green light, Malaki would resent him. Commander Sanchez had learned long ago, when a man made up his mind to do something, there was nothing you could do about it. "Malaki, my son. You know you are my heartbeat?"

"Yes, Papa."

"Son, I have trained you and given you all that I can give to prepare you for your journey. You do know if you don't succeed what your outcome will be?"

Malaki nodded his head in understanding. What was understood needs no explaining.

"Malaki. If you feel you are ready to spill the blood of your parents' killer, then son, who am I to tell you, you are not?"

"I am ready, Papa."

Commander Sanchez pulled Malaki into his warm embrace. A tear fell from his eye. "Then son, go."

"I will return, Papa. I promise you." Malaki said hugging his father.

Commander Sanchez knew it was a 50-50 chance he would see his son alive again. After releasing Malaki, he wiped his tears, took a pull from his Cuban and blew the smoke out. "Malaki, make me proud."

"I will, Papa. I will." Malaki vowed and went to pack his things. He had a flight to catch. In a few days he would be touching down in the most violent city in the country. His training would be tested in the battlefield. He would let nothing stop him while he unleashed hell in the city of murder and mayhem.

***

Mr. Biggs sat at his desk inside his immaculate mansion on the outskirts of Chicago overlooking Lake Michigan. For the past 20 years he had dominated and controlled the drug trade in the Midwest with his hand stretching as far as Vancouver, Canada. He was getting old but when he stepped in the deadly game of murder and drugs he vowed that he would die a boss and the king of the underworld. He had enough money and real estate to retire from the game and live lavishly for the rest of his life, but he was addicted to life. He could never walk away from the game; it has been good for him. He was infatuated with the power to end another man's life with the nod of a head, the extravagant cars and homes, and women was intoxicating, and he wouldn't trade it for anything in the world.

After robbing Castilino for 1,000 kilos of uncut heroin it was no turning back. He had ordered Castilino's death but his man had missed and that mistake left with his life. With money and power, Mr. Biggs had an army of killers at his disposal willing to kill anything moving in the name of Mr. Biggs and the Body Snatcher Nation. He could care less about Castilino or his cartel. To him, the Cartel was nothing more than a bunch of peasant farmers who used Americans like himself to move their dope. While the Americans took the risk and awoke with Federal nightmares, they stayed across the border reaping the benefits and getting filthy rich. He knew Castilino was over-charging him for the heroin, and then on top of that, Castelino would put him on hold for periods at a time blaming it on the war he was fighting against rival cartels. Mr. Biggs hated waiting on others in order for his riches and foundation to grow. He wanted to be his own boss. After robbing Castelino, it was game over and now he was getting his bricks from the Africans overseas. Allowing him to control the game and everything in it.

Mr. Biggs looked over at his security camera and saw Killa Fred's silver Range Rover pulling into the driveway and park behind his Cadillac Escalade. Watching Killa Fred hop out the whip he hoped they had some good news for him about the Peter Gunz situation. Peter Gunz had tested his gangster so his execution was ordered in order to protect his reputation in the dope game. Feeling his iPhone 6 vibrate in his pocket. He already knew it was Butter calling to let him know his henchman had just arrived. Butter was his chief enforcer for his security detail.

"Send them in." Mr. Biggs said answering his phone. A minute later there was a knock at the door. "Come in."

Killa Fred and Body Bag entered the office. Body Bag had a blunt of Kush hanging from his dry lips and a large duffle bag slung over his shoulder.

"What's good big homie?" Killa Fred shook Mr. Biggs' hand before he sat down on the plush leather sofa.

"Samn ol', some ol'. Y'all got some good news for me?"

"Old School, you already know how we do." Body Bag stated, put the large duffle bag on Mr. Biggs' desk and then passed the blunt to Killa Fred.

"That's what I like to hear, youngster," Mr. Bigg replied while proceeding to unzip the duffle bag. Looking in the bag, Mr. Biggs jumped back. "Man, what the fuck!" was his only reply before Body Bag started laughing. "You niggaz is crazy. What the fuck is wrong with you sick muthafuckers!" Mr. Biggs was in shook as he looked in the dead eyes of Peter Gunz's decapitated skull.

"You said make a statement and that's what we did." Body Bag replied and went to retrieve the head that was wrapped in plastic.

Killa Fred just shook his head. He knew Body Bag was on some bullshit the minute he ran back into the mansion, but when he came back with Peter Gunz's head he knew Body Bag had lost his mind. He was the devil in the flesh.

"How much is in the bag?" Mr. Biggs asked shaking off the initial shock of seeing Peter Gunz's decapitated.

Killa Fred passed the weed to Me. Biggs who inhaled it like it was his last. "It's supposed to be like 2-mill. Not sure though."

Mr. Biggs let the weed entered his bloodstream and relax him before he spoke. "I told you. It's not about the money. But the respect. Y'all keep the money." Mr. Biggs blew the thick Kush smoke through his nostrils.

A smile spread across Killa Fred face. He knew Mr. Biggs would let them walk with the cash.

"Y'all take the money and the head. Get up outta here. I have something to take care of. And take that sick mutherfucker with you." Mr. Biggs pointed at Body Bag.

Killa Fred and Body Bag stood up. Body Bag put the human head back in the bag and zipped it. "I'll give you a call tomorrow boss." Killa Fred said as him and Body Bag walked out the office.

Mr. Biggs watched as the killas left with 2 mill and a human skull. He knew now more than ever that his Body Snatchers was nothing to be fucked with.

S. Allen

Chapter 4

Malaki's plane landed in Chicago, Illinois on a Friday night at Midwest Airport. It was his first time riding a plane. The flight was somewhat relaxing. He told the driver to take him to the Congress Hotel in downtown Chicago.

Commander Sanchez provided him with a blueprint to enter his deadly mission in revenge. Malaki had a fake ID as well as a fake bank account with $50,000 in cash and multiple bogus credit cards. Driving in downtown Chicago Malaki was intrigued by the tall buildings in his sight. He had only seen such structures on TV and in magazines. He was a little nervous to say the least. The cross streets were something new to him, but all nervousness subsided on the thoughts of his parents being killed on these same cold streets.

The cab driver pulled up to the front of the Congress Hotel and parked at the curb. "That will be $25, my boy." He said in his strong Haitian accent.

Malaki pulled out a wad of money and pulled off two twenties. "Keep the change."

"Thank you, my brother. Welcome to Chicago."

Malaki nodded at the river, grabbed his luggage and exited the cab. After walking into the exclusive hotel, Malaki approached the desk.

"Welcome to the Congress Hotel, how can I help you?" The receptionist at the desk asked with a warm smile.

"Yo, reservation for Henry Jones." Malaki replied returning a smile of his own.

"Just one minute, sir." The receptionist began typing on the computer until she stumbled upon what she was looking for. "Yes, we do have one room for you, Mr. Jones. How will you be paying? Cash or credit?"

"Credit." Malaki handed her his fake ID and a bogus American Express credit card. A few moments later he was handed the keys to his presidential suite.

"If you need anything, Mr. Jones— I do mean anything— please call the front desk and ask for Vicki." The receptionist flirted.

"I'll keep that in mind, Vicki." Malaki walked inside his suite and was astonished by how immaculate it was.

The room was lavish. A king size canopy bed occupied the bedroom as well as a 60-inch flat screen TV. Malaki laid on the plush bed and put his hands behind his head. It had been a long flight and he had been up for the last 18 hours and was in dying need of some rest. He figured he would get a few winks in.

A knock at the door disturbed him from his light nap. After jumping up from the bed, he answered the door. "Who is it?" Malaki said visibly irritated.

"Delivery for Mr. Jones, from the front desk." The bellboy said on the other side of the door. Malaki opened the door to see the bellboy holding a huge box that was marked UPS. "Sign here, sir."

Malaki signed for the package before going back to his room. The package had been sent from South Dakota. He had been expecting it since his plane landed in the Chi. After opening the box, he pulled out a porcelain statue of Buddha, a note was taped to his belly. Malaki grabbed the note and read it.

My son, if you're reading this scribe then you have already completed the first part of your mission. Remember, Malaki. Keep your eyes and your ears open at all times and trust nothing but your heart. Move like the soldier you are and trust your instincts. You are new in the battlefield and about to declare war on your enemies. In order to conquer the jungle, you must be the predator. Never let yourself become the prey.

Malaki soaked in his father's words of wisdom like a sponge. He knew he had to play offense if he had any chances of surviving what he was about to engage; he couldn't be faking. He reached in the box and pulled out a small hammer that was sent with the package. After striking the statue twice it crumbled into pieces.

Inside the statue rested a 10-millimeter Glock, two twenty shot clips as well as a silencer. Malaki stacked the clip in the bottom of the Glock and pulled the slide back, chambering a round into the cold chamber. Feeling the automatic in his hands gave him a warm embrace. He was willing and ready to hunt his enemies down and leave them bleeding in the streets.

Malaki learned through doing his homework that a lot of the big-time drug dealers in Chicago partied at a strip club called the King of Diamonds on the southside of the city. He couldn't seem to understand the logic of risking your life in the drug game, and then throwing it all the way on strippers. In his militant mind it didn't make sense. In all reality it wasn't for him to understand, he wasn't in the business of dealing drugs. He was trained assassin in the business of dealing death. Malaki went in his suitcase and pulled out a few bundles of cash. After counting a bankroll of $50,000 he began to plot for tomorrow. It would be Saturday and he would need a few tools before he started his mission. The first thing in the morning he would head to a car lot to purchase a vehicle. Next, he would go shopping for some new gear. If he wanted to get close to Mr. Biggs and the Body Snatchers he would have to play his part and look to a part of their world. The world of money and drugs. Malaki studied a few rappers like Meek Mill, Yo Gotti and Jeezy to see how they dressed and what brands they wore. His swag had to be on point if he had any chance of serving Mr. Biggs his death warrant. He was about to hit the streets of Chicago like a Tycoon. When he was finished the whole city would have felt his wrath.

Poncho sat in his secluded apartment on the city's Northside putting shells in the clip of his FNH pistol. He had been doing surveillance on the Body Snatcher Organization for the last year. He was on a one-way mission to kill the boss of the crime family. Mr. Biggs. Poncho had been sent from Juarez, Mexico to complete a murder contract for his boss. "El Senor" Castillo Medina.

Poncho Guemez was born and raised on the war-stricken streets of Juarez, Mexico just across the border of El Paso, Texas. His family was poor like most of the residents of Juarez. When he was only five years of age, Poncho's father was kidnapped by an evil drug cartel known as the Los-Tecca to work in the opium fields. The Los Texas controlled the small city of Juarez with the mission to be their own government. Poncho's mother was now dismissed with her husband gone from their home. With no money or food, young Poncho took to the streets to steal ss a means of survival. It was at that time he adopted his do or die attitude in life.

At 15 years old Poncho started to see a change in his city. An up and coming drug lord by the name of Castilino Madina felt that Juarez had enough of the Los-Tecca and their sinister politics and decided to start his own drug cartel. The Medina Cartel. The mayor of Juarez was being extorted by the Los-Terrawho only used him for his political ties and influence. The mayor backed Castilino, giving him the connection and support needed to put him in the position of power. Eventually Castilino went to war with the Los-Tecca over control of the cocaine and heroin distribution into the United States.

Poncho's father saw a chance to escape from the Los-Tecca slavery. His attempt was futile. Shortly after his escape he was caught and beheaded. Poncho found his father's head on his porch as he came home from playing soccer with some friends. The hate he conjured in his heart for the Los-Tecca was unreal. Young Poncho went to the Medina Cartel pleading to join in their quest to rid the Los-Tecca from Juarez. The cartel wasted no time recruiting the young demon. With his violent attitude and bloodthirst, Poncho climbed the ranks of the Medina Cartel. Trained as an assassin and at only 25, Poncho had 30 bodies under his belt. All high-ranking members of the Los-Tecca. Castilino saw his wrath within the Cartel and only used Poncho for certain missions, which is why he was sent to Chicago to dismantle the Body Snatchers and put Mr. Biggs in the ground before the attempt on his life.

The 6,000 kilos were of no importance. Mr. Biggs would die for his disrespect.

Poncho figured the hit would be quick and deadly, and he would be back across the border in less than a week. He was wrong. Mr. Biggs had a vicious army of killers that would murder at his beckoning call. His security was always tight and Mr. Biggs moved through the city like he was the president. Poncho caught Mr. Biggs a few times. But never slipping, he was always with his killers and in the eyes of the public. In due time, time would present itself, and when it did Poncho would be ready. Tonight, he would continue to do surveillance in hopes he would be able to execute the biggest drug lord in the Midwest.

Chapter 5

Malaki caught a cab to Zimbrick and Buick car lot on Western Street and was now on the lot looking for a whip. Malaki stopped and was admiring a navy-blue Buick Lacrosse.

"You like what you see, young man?" The short, chubby salesman asked; his Giorgio Armani looking expensive.

"How much for the car?" Malaki replied liking the peanut butter interior.

"This right here son is the best Buick has to offer. Bose system and 20-inch tires, this right here. Base Price $40,000."

Malaki walked around the car, his hands in his army fatigue cargo pants. "I'll take it."

The white salesmen looked at Malaki suspiciously giving him a once over. "Alright then, right this way. We can start the paperwork immediately." He saw Malaki pulling the bands of cash from his pockets.

After 45 minutes Malaki pulled out of the parking lot, his body sunk into the seats of Lacrosse as the car drove smoothly over the potholed streets of the city. Spending $10,000 in cash he left the mall with Gucci, Loui, and Tru Religion. Tonight, he was going to the King of Diamonds to see if he could spot the infamous Mr. Biggs.

It was 10:00 at night. Pancho slumped in the driver's seat of his Range Rover behind a set of binoculars. A cigar hung from his lips. He had been ducked off in the cut before the club opened its doors, that way he could see who came and went. Three black and white photos rested on his las. One of Mr. Biggs, one of Killa Fred and one of the Psychopath. Body Bag. Every time a foreign whip pulled up poncho would get tense, gaining his adversaries had arrived at the club. Poncho grabbed his gun and patiently waited.

Malaki pulled into the parking lot at the King of Diamonds strip club. It was almost 12:30 and the club was packed. Different kinds of expensive whips flooded the parking lot— Range Rovers, Benz, Audis, and Bentleys just to name a few. He slid the Buick through the lot and parked on the side of the club so he could get away if things went haywire. After stepping out the car Malaki hit the alarm on his key chain to lock it. At first Malaki opted to take the Glock with him, but then decided against it and left it under the driver's seat for easy access. While standing in the line of the club he was approached by a thick redbone sista. He was fresh to death in a black Gucci jean outfit, Prada leather loafers covering his feet while a 32-inch platinum chain hung from his neck. The Issey Miyake cologne graced the air of all who was around him.

"Damn sexy what's your name?" The redbone asked showing her cleavage. Her Dereon jeans looked to be as if they were painted on her curvaceous frame.

Malaki looked her up and down. She was a brick house in every meaning of the word, but he wasn't at the club to socialize, he was in war mode and had only one thing on his mind. Murder.

"Damn boy you can't hear?" The redbone asked.

Malaki continued to ignore her advanced while he paid the $10.00 cover charge to get in the club.

"Must be a homo thug." Redbone seethed under her breath.

Inside, the small club was packed to capacity. The smell of sweat, cheap perfume and weed smoke evaded the air. Malaki watched as a thick stripper with tattoos on her ass slid down the pole and started popping her pussy. The ballers on the front row of the stage threw dollar bills and made it rain all over the dancers. Malaki scanned the faces of the men at the stage. He knew the faces he was looking for; he had seen the faces countless times in his dreams and nightmares. His photogenic memory was flawless. The sounds of Future banged from the club's speakers, vibrating the wall of the club. Malaki approached the bar and took a seat.

The chocolate skinned waiter asked, "What can I get you sexy?" Her only piece of clothing a black Victoria's Secret thong.

"A Pepsi." Malaki replied.

"Coming right up sweetie." The whore walked off to fix Malaki's drink, ass juggling with each step.

Malaki turned around continuing to watch the crowd.

"Check out homie with the shines on," Brisco said to his patna Murda after he downed his shot of Tequila.

Murda looked in the direction of Malaki and saw his platinum chain shining from all the way in the back of the club. Brisco and Murda were from the Westside of Chicago. They were known jack boys who specialized in robbing and kidnapping drug dealers and tonight was just another night on the job.

"You see 'em come in with anybody?"

"Nope. I think homie by himself. Came to the club solo." Brisco said rubbing his hands together, anticipating the lick.

"I'll be right back fam." Murda stood up and walked toward the bar.

Malaki had just paid for his drink when the skinny dark-skinned dude with dreads approached the bar.

"Let me get a bottle of Cîroc!" The guy yelled to the bartender over the loud music. Pulling out a large wad of bills he gave Malaki a onceover. Malaki took a sip of his soda. "What's good, family? This bitch crackin' tonight ain't it?" Murda said trying to strike up a convo with Malaki.

Malaki looked at him and nodded. Murda was dripping in ice. The waiter came back and gave him his bottle.

"You from the Chi?" Murda asked as he took a swig from the Cîroc.

"No." Malaki responded watching the stripper on the stage.

"Who you affiliated with, my nigga?" Murda wanted to know if Malaki was involved in gang activity before he made his move.

Malaki turned to face Murda. "Listen, I'm trying to talk to Mr. Biggs. Do you know where I can find him?" Malaki asked with no emotion at all.

Murda looked at him with his head cocked to the side. Whoever this dude was in front of him was looking for the boss of all bosses. Murda knew exactly who Mr. Biggs was. Mr. Biggs and the Body Snatchers flooded the city with drugs. He tried to fuck with Mr. Biggs on the business tip and get on but they knew his reputation as a stick-up kid and never gave him any dealings. So, he continued to eat the only way he knew how. With the steel. "Naw, fam. Never heard of him." Murda lied, walking off leaving Malaki at the bar.

S. Allen

"What's up with scud?" Brisco asked when Murda returned to the table.

"Nigga asking about Biggs."

"Straight up? Think he the Feds?"

"I doubt it. He got that out of town swag. He might be trying to cop some work from them niggas."

"So, what we gonna do?"

"When he hit the parking lot, we gone follow him to his whip and poke his ass." Murda took a drink of Cîroc.

"That's what I'm talking about. Fuck he think this is? This Chi-Raq," was Brisco's only reply.

After two hours at the Club Malaki couldn't identify any of his targets he had come to eliminate nor had he found any info pointing him in the direction of Mr. Biggs or his cronies. He learned that speaking Mr. Biggs' name in the streets was like speaking about Lucifer himself. The lights in the club came on indicating that the club was at its closing time. Malaki walked outside and stood in front of the club scanning the crowd one last time before he walked to his vehicle.

Poncho was behind his binoculars focusing on the front of the club as the party goers exited. I was a little past 2 in the morning. A lot of gangsters, dealers and pimps lingered in front of the establishment trying to get at some of the strippers leaving the club. A man in all black was walking through the parking lot. What piqued his interest were the two men that was following him. One of the men seemed to be holding something behind his back, resembling some kind of firearm.

Malaki hit the alarm on his key chain. The headlights on the Buick blinked twice. Malaki's Spidey Senses were alerted. He noticed the two men following him. The same guy who approached him at the bar. Malaki's main objective was to get to his gun. The footsteps were closer and closer.

"Aye fam let us holler at you real quick." Murda sneered.

Malaki looked back and was now face to face with the barrel of a 40 caliber.

"Lets us get that chain playa." Brisco hissed through clenched teeth.

Malaki sized up the amateurs. They underestimated him and that mistake would cost me gravely.

"Okay. I don't want any trouble." Malaki put his hands up in a surrendering motion.

Brisco went for the chain on Malaki's neck. Malaki smiled and then side-swept to the left grabbing Brisco's wrist and the side of the 40 at the same time. After pulling the slide back of the gun and dissecting it from its frame, he slung it, leaving Brisco holding only half of the weapon in his hand. Murda attempted to grab Malaki but was met with a punch to the center of his throat. Gasping for air Murda fell to his knees holding his throat.

Malaki still holding Brisco's broken wrist in his hand spun around him and snapped his neck. A loud snapping noise filled the air. Brisco was dead before he hit the cement. Murda was still gasping for air when Malaki walked over and gave him the same issue as his man. A broken neck. Without breaking his stride Malaki got in his car and pulled off, leaving the two thugs as dead as a doorknob.

Poncho watched the violence play out in awe. The man who had just put the work in was not your average street thug. The whole incident took 60 seconds. He watched as the man pulled off into the night. Starting up the Range Rover Poncho pulled out of the lot behind the Lacrosse. The man was somebody, and he had to find who that somebody was.

S. Allen

Chapter 6

Ronnie and his cousin Lil' Tony were in a trap spot in the Englewood area of the Southside. Ten kilos of uncut heroin sat at the front table in front of them. The two dope pushers were scheduled to drop the bricks off in Kansas City in two days. Killa Fred had just one of his lieutenants drop the work off to them. Ronnie and Lil' Tony were first cousins and they had been with the Body Snatchers for the past 3 years. Ronnie had been a foot soldier for the Gangster Disciples before Mr. Biggs and his crew brought war to the Disciples and responded, taking over their drug turf. Ronnie switched sides as soon as the bullets flew his way. Since rotating with the Body Snatchers Ronnie's bank roll had begun to flourish. He started seeing money he never saw with the Disciples. A few months later Ronnie's cousin Lil' Tony jumped on board. Killa Fred was their superior and they answered to him and only him. He put the two dealers in a position to do well for themselves. Their staff titles and duties were to drop off kilos of heroin to out-of-town clientele. The payment for them was $2,500 off each kilo delivered. Ronnie was greedy and felt he should be getting more money since he was taking all of the risk. And his greed got the best of him.

"Man, we need to stop cutting these bricks and serve them how they are." Lil' Tony said as he watched Ronnie unwrap one of the bricks and break it down.

"What the fuck is wrong with you, cuz? We taking all these federal ass chances hitting these highways for a pound at $10,000 a move, while these niggas laying up in mansions, driving Porsche trucks and shit!"

Lil' Tony shook his head. He knew what they were doing was wrong, and if they were ever caught, they would pay for it with their lives.

"What the fuck? You just gone sit there twiddling your thumbs? Unwrap me one of the bricks so we can get this done and over with."

Lil' Tony hesitantly grabbed one of the kilos and started to unwrap the plastic. His gut feeling was telling him what they were doing would fall back in their laps.

The two dealers proceeded to break down and remix the drugs. For every 36 ounces of heroin Ronnie would cut 9 ounces and replace it with 9 ounces of Milk Surfer. What was 85% of heroin was now only 65%. They had 10 kilos of dope, and after the procedure was done, Ronnie and Lil' Tony would have 90 ounces of uncut dope. After they completed the demonstration Ronnie used a compressor to rebrick the kilos, and then rewrapped them. It took them four hours to complete the process. Both were tired as the fumes from the narcotics polluted the air.

"Let's get up outta here fam." Ronnie stated stuffing the last kilos inside a leather Gucci bag. They had a long ride to Kansas City. The quicker they got back to the Chi, the quicker they could move the work.

Body Bag slid his new Mercedes SL550 down the Dan Ryan Expressway. The car he had just got was fresh off the showroom floor and cost him 85 racks, and Body Bag was feeling himself. At only 26 years old he had the world at his feet. Being Mr. Biggs' enforcer had paved the way for him, and with his violent tactics he was the most feared gangster in the City of Chicago since the late "Pops" Johnson. Body Bag was headed to a drug area on the Westside ran by the Body Snatchers. The spot on Chicago Avenue was coming up short on the weekly profit and Body Bag was coming to check and see what the problem was.

Body Bag got off on Independence Street and entered the violent neighborhood of the city. Turning down Chicago Avenue he saw a flock of young thugs posted on the corner. The sight of dope fiends in a single file line in the middle of the block let Body Bag know that the money was definitely coming in. After parking behind a beat-up van, Body Bag scanned the block through the tent of his Benz. Opening his glove compartment, he retrieved his . 44 revolver and stuck the large cannon on his waistline. The house he was going in was the money house; the house all the dope money was kept.

Body Bag stepped out of the Benz. His long dreads falling past his shoulders while his diamond chain hung over his black Prada hoodie. Walking up on the porch of the crib he left the car running.

He dared anybody to come close to his whip. The thugs in the neighborhood knew him as well as his murderous reputation. The loud sounds of Twista banged from the other side of the door.

Body Bag pounded on the door four times. After a minute nobody came to the door, so he banged again, his irritation growing by the minute. He was about to kick the door in until it came open.

A young, light skinned female stood on the other side. "Excuse me, can I help you?" She said with much attitude.

Body Bag gave her a sinister look before he sneered. "Bitch, you can start by moving the fuck out my way." He shoved her to the side, closing the door behind him.

Terry, who was supposed to be on point, came from the back room zipping up his Tru Religion jeans, a blunt of Kush hanging from his lips. "What's good big homie? Didn't knew that was you knocking."

Body Bag scanned the living room and saw two more workers and a few females sitting on the couch. A bottle of Patron was on the table along with blunt wrappers. The two workers immediately stood up. Terry turned the stereo off.

"Y'all bitches get the fuck out!" Body Bag said; his eyes bloodshot red. That two chicks remained seated like they were hard of hearing. Body Bag pulled the chrome cannon from his jeans and cocked it. The two females jumped off the couch like fire was lit to their asses and made a B-Line through the front door. Light skin in tow.

"My fault big homie." Terry tried to plea.

Body Bag swung the large cannon, connecting it with Terry's jaw. The loud crunching sound from his jaw being broken could be heard throughout the house. "So that's why my money ain't coming up right? Because y'all stupid mutherfuckers over here having a house party instead of standing on the business?" Body Bag said through clenched teeth.

Terry spat out 3 of his teeth.

"You motherfuckers get paid to count money. Nothing more. Nothing less. This block been coming up short in the last few weeks. Pick up is tomorrow. If so much as a penny came up short of the bread, niggas better have some life insurance because your people gone be planning y'all funeral." Body Bag looked into the petrified faces of his workers, and to make sure his words were set in stone he aimed the gun at Terry's leg and pulled the trigger. *Boooom!*

Terry let out a piercing scream as he clutched his leg and fell to the floor. Blood poured from his gunshot wound profusely.

"Now get this motherfucker to a hospital." Body Bag left the house with a smoking gun. After jumping back in his Benz he pulled off. He had to be in Kansas City by morning and didn't have time to be wasting.

The Next Day

Beep-Beep. Ronnie watched as the last five stacks ran through the money machine. He grabbed the stack of bills, placed a thick red rubber band around it and placed it in the duffle bag. Ronnie, Lil' Tony and Jabo had just counted 175,000 dead presidents.

Jobo stood from the table and stretched. "Goddamn, whoever thought counting money could make you tired?"

"Nigga you ain't did nothing. The machine did all the work." Ronnie replied zipping up the duffle bag full of cash.

Jabo examined one of the bricks on the table. "So, this the last work from last time right?"

"Why wouldn't it be?" Ronnie retorted.

"Naw, I'm just asking fam, because that shit last time was off the chain. I was able to cut it 6 times and it was still a nook."

"Well if you moving like that, you should be coping more than 10, don't you think?" Ronnie said with a raised eyebrow, slinging the duffle bag over his shoulder.

"Yea. I probably got 20 on the next re-up."

Ronnie was already doing the numbers in his head. *180 ounces of pure D*, a smile plastered his greedy face. "You already know. Just get at us."

Ronnie and Lil' Tony left Kansas City headed back to Chicago to turn in the money to Killa Fred and then hustle their own work.

The money was about to start coming by the boatload. So he thought.

When Ronnie and Lil' Tony left, Jabo called out to Body Bag who emerged from the back room firing up a blunt of Sour Diesel. Jabo threw him one of the kilos, which he caught with one hand. After examining the brick, he smiled. He knew just by looking at the drugs that it had been tampered with.

"So, what's the demo?" Jabo asked grabbing the count from Body Bag.

"These niggas playing a vicious game, that's the demo. They so stupid they didn't even re-stamp the work." The Body Snatchers' bricks all had the stamp of the grim reaper on each and every kilo.

"What you gone do with the work?"

"Keep it. Bring me back a 100 geez."

Jabo had just came up. He knew he would make well over a 100 grand. "That's a bet big homie, I'll give you a call when I'm done flipping this shit."

"Yea. You do that." Body Bag left Kansas City, Missouri on his way back to the Chi. The $175,000 had been Mr. Biggs' own money. Killa Fred had suspected some foul play with Ronnie and Lil' Tony tampering with the work and had devised a plan to see if indeed that was the case. They failed the test and was caught red handed. Stealing from the Body Snatchers was inexcusable and punishable by death. Body Bag put the Benz in cruise control. When he got back on land he would take care of the two cousins, ASAP. Thoughts of murder took over his mind as he headed back to the battlefield.

S. Allen

Chapter 7

Malaki sat in his plush residential suite reading a copy of the Chicago Tribune. Commander Sanchez had always told him the news was the key to information. While looking in the local section of the paper he was shocked to see that they had information about the two bodies he caught at the strip club. Malaki read the article

Two men found dead in parking lot at a southside gentlemen's club. 22 year old Jarvis Black and 26 year old Corey Simms were found dead in the parking lot of the King of Diamonds strip club. Police say witnesses called the bodies in at 2:45 Sunday morning. The two men were found unresponsive by what appears to be a dislocation of the neck and spinal cord. Jarvis Black who had an extensive criminal record with charges of armed robbery to felony murder had just been released from Menard Penitentiary, while 26 year old Cory Simms was on parole for aggravated robbery. Police have no suspects at this time.

Malaki tossed the newspaper to the side. He hadn't been in Chicago 48 hours and had already killed two men with his bare hands. He didn't know who the men were, but they came at him aggressively, so he responded to the situation like he was supposed to. With aggression.

He still didn't have a lead on Mr. Biggs or the Body Snatchers. Within a city with over 2 million people, finding Mr. Biggs would be like searching for a needle in a haystack. Malaki vowed he would not rest until he spilled his enemies' blood. Today was a new day and with new opportunities. It was raining outside, and the sky was dark over the city. His food supply was limited, and he was tired of ordering room service. Malaki put on his jacket and slid the Glock on his waist and headed out the door to hit a restaurant.

The rain continued to pour extensively as the windshield wipers swiped repeatedly on the windshield of the Dodge Challenger as Poncho watched the Buick Lacrosse he had been trailing. Ever since the incident at the strip club he had been interested in finding out who the man was that caused the mayhem. He hadn't seen such brutality since Mexico. Poncho watched the man's moves closely and knew that his fighting style was of mixed martial arts, but the dissection of the firearm was something of a different league. The man was either Military Special OPS or a trained killer. Whatever the case he had to find out. For all he knew, the man could have been trying to bring him a move before he was attacked. Poncho had filled so many murder contracts that he had enemies all over the country. That's how it was living the life of an assassin.

Poncho grabbed his cell phone and dialed a number. "Hola, El-Senor."

"Como estas, my friend."

"Just checking in, Senor Medina."

"How is everything going?"

"As of the moment I am getting close to eliminating the target. But I have run into something that I have very much interest in."

"What is that?" Castilino questioned.

"This man. I think he is following me. But I'm not sure."

"Why would you say that?"

"I see this man in action. Two men attacked him and he disarmed them and put them down with much finesse."

Castilino let out a small chuckle. "If you feel this man is a threat then you must eliminate that threat, my son."

Poncho thought hard before he spoke. "I will see what's to this man, El-Senor."

"Whatever you decide to do. Make sure you complete the mission. I do not want Mr. Biggs and his thugs breathing the same air as me. Do I make myself clear?"

"I will have him on the ground soon." Poncho replied watching the front of the Congress Hotel.

"That's what I like to hear." Castilino terminated the call.

After putting the phone back in his pocket, Poncho continued to watch the mystery man emerge from the front door of the hotel. Watching him through his binoculars he saw the man jumped in his vehicle and pull off. Poncho turned the key in the ignition, bringing the SUV to life, and pulled out of the parking lot following his target through the grimy streets of Chicago. He had come up with a plan, and when the time came he would put it all in motion.

Standing in line at the Harold's Chicken Shack on 87th Street, Malaki waited to get the six-piece dinner he had just ordered. Malaki found out about the exclusive restaurant through a commercial and figured he would give their fried chicken a try. Malaki was told that his order would take 15 minutes, so he patiently waited.

Seeing Malaki get out his car and enter the restaurant, Poncho knew it was time to take care of business and pulled into the parking lot of Harold's Chicken. Parking his whip, he grabbed his 357 Python and exited the vehicle.

"Thank you," Malaki said as the lady in the restaurant gave him his order. The smell of fried chicken was overwhelming, and he couldn't wait to get to the car. As hungry as he was, he knew he had no chance at making it back to the hotel. He was going to punish the food, ASAP. Malaki hit the alarm on his key chain and got in. Putting the chicken in the passenger seat he attempted to start the car until he felt something hard and cold press up against the back of his skull.

"Put your hands up, Eśe. Nice and slow." Poncho sneered with ice dripping from his tone. Malaki thought about reaching for his weapon. Poncho cocked the hammer on the 357 reading Malaki's thoughts. "I'll be taking this. my friend." Poncho relieved Malaki of the Glock on his waist.

"What do you want?" Malaki asked while still trying to formulate a plan to get him out of the situation.

"For starters, I want you to start the car and pull off. If you try anything funny, I will put your brains on the dashboard. Comprende, amigo?" Poncho was calm as he gave his orders.

Malaki put the car in drive and pulled out of the parking lot. "What do you want?" Malaki asked again trying to get a feel for his abductor.

"I want to know who you are."

"Why is that important? Do you want money?" Malaki stopped at a red light.

"No, my friend. I want you to make a left on the next street. If you fail to meet my request, you die."

Malaki did as he was told and made a left on State Street. Lake Michigan was visible even though the rain poured down with dramatic intent.

"Turn here." Pocho commanded nudging Malaki with the cold steel.

Malaki turned down a street that led to the 35th Street beach. The parking lot was dark and empty. For the entire ride he had been trying to come up with a play that would save his life. He knew that the man who kidnapped him was serious, due to how calm he was.

"Park right here and slowly turn off the car."

Malaki did as he was told.

"I ask you again. Who are you?"

Malaki remained stone-faced and silent.

"You tough guy, huh, amigo? Get out now."

Malaki proceed to exit the car while Poncho did the same. The split second was all that Malaki needed to make his move. He roundhouse kicked which caught Poncho off guard, while he was attempting to get out of the car, and at the same time grabbed the revolver in Poncho's hand, put his finger on the trigger, making the gun bark six times, emptying the cannon.

Poncho released a vicious leg sweep that put Malaki on his back. "You stupid Americans." Poncho growled and pulled the trigger again, only to come up with a click, click. The chamber was spent. Poncho slung the weapon to the ground and turned his head down trying to crush Malaki's skull.

After grabbing Poncho's ankle Malaki twisted it, causing Poncho to fall to the ground. Malaki stood up in a fighting position, as did Poncho. The thunder cracked in the dark sky.

"Who are you?"

"Your worst nightmare." Malaki replied and released a fury of punch and kick combinations.

Poncho blocked all but one. A punch to the bridge of his nose. "Jiu Jitsu, huh?" Poncho said wiping the blood that was coming from his nose.

Malaki attacked again but this time Poncho anticipated it. He side-swiped to the left and caught Malaki with a knee to the rib cage, and then a punch to the jaw. Malaki shook off the blow as he held his aching jawbone.

"Who are you?" Poncho repeated before he released his own assault, trying to end Malaki. The two assassins fought until both were out of breath. Neither wanting to fall victim. "You fight well, amigo," Poncho replied kneeling now.

"What do you want from me? If I tell you my name, will you leave me in peace?"

"Yes, my friend. You tell me who you are, I will let you be."

Malaki wiped the blood from his swollen lips. "You know I could've killed you, right?"

Poncho stood up and laughed at Malaki's statements before he pulled Malaki's Glock 10 from his waist and pointed in Malaki's direction. "I could've taken your life. Leave your brains on the pavement, amigo." Poncho released the magazine, pulled the slide back, ejecting the 10-millimeter round from the chamber and tossed the Glock to Malaki.

Malaki snatched the weapon from the air.

"Now who are you?" Poncho asked, tossing him the clip to the gun.

"My name is Malaki. Why didn't you use the gun?"

"I didn't use the Hun because my intent was not to kill you, I wanted to see how well you were trained. Are you ex-military? Who do you work for?"

"I'm here in Chicago to avenge my parents' murders." Malaki stuck the gun in the small of his back.

"I feel sorry for those putas. You fight well, my friend."

"Who are you and why did you follow me?" Malaki inquired.

"My name is Poncho, I'm from Mexico. I am also on a mission for revenge. I followed you because I thought you were following me. I am a killer looking for my enemies."

"I'm looking for Mr. Biggs. Do you know where I can find him?" Malaki asked stepping toward Poncho.

Poncho looked at Malaki in disbelief. "Why do you look for this Mr. Biggs, amigo?"

"So I can kill him. That's why." There was a moment of intense silence.

"Malaki, I think we need to talk."

"Talk about what?"

"Bringing Mr. Biggs his death." Malaki was confused. Poncho noticed it. "My friend, follow me and I will tell you all the information you need to bring the end of Mr. Biggs."

Malaki didn't have a lead on Mr. Biggs or his cronies, and him running around hoping and praying to stumble upon the drug lord was not working. If Poncho could bring him remotely close to Mr. Biggs he would be willing to take that chance. If Poncho showed any signs of betrayal he would blow his brains out. Point-blank-period. Malaki nodded his head in agreement.

"Wise choice, my friend." Poncho said and hopped into the passenger's side of Malaki's whip. Malaki stood for a minute analyzing the situation.

"Fuck it!" He said to himself. It was do or die.

Chapter 8

Body Bag sat low in the seat of his tinted Dodge Magnum. Jay-Z's The Streets is Watching pumped low from the factory speakers inside the whip. It was 3:00 in the morning and his target still hadn't come home. Watching the house located on the Westside, a 223 assault rifle rested on his lap. Killa Fred had ordered the murders of Ronnie and Lil' Tony sending Body Bag as the messenger of death. For most niggas in the game, killing was a fashion trend. But to him it was a lifestyle. He had a thirst for blood, and every time an opportunity presented itself, he would perform and quench his thirst. For every mission he went on, somebody died. All except one. The hit on Castilino Medina. The Cartel Boss. The failed attempt constantly stayed on his mental. Body Bag grabbed a Kush blunt from the ashtray and lit it. He took a strong pull from the exotic weed and let his mind drift to the Castilino hit.

He remembered it like it was just yesterday. Castilio had told Mr. Biggs that the 100-kilo supply of uncut heroin would be on hold 'til further notice. The Medina Cartel and the Los-Tecca were engaged in a bloody turf war in Mexico, over the pipelines used to transport drugs into the United States. In the midst of the drug war Castilino had the authorities on his back, and he wanted to slow down his distribution to focus on his enemies. Mr. Biggs felt some kind of way as he was down to his last few kilos. Castilino told Mr. Biggs it was no way he was sending anything into the United States at that time and to be patient. Mr. Biggs, being at the peak of his power in Chicago, wanted Castilino dead and began to plot his demise. Mr. Biggs wanted the Body Snatchers to be the powerhouse at the drug game on a nationwide level, and the opportunity would be a transfer of power.

Mr. Bigg contacted the Cartel Boss and told him he had 40-million in cold cash and wanted to place an order. Castilino was giving Mr. Biggs the kilo for S40,000 a brick. So, for a cool $40-million, Biggs was asking for 1,000 kilos. It was the biggest order Castilino would ever fill. And the $40-million would put him in helluva financial gain, and would help buy more guns and recruit more soldiers to fight against Los Tecca. At first Castilino was curious as if Mr. Biggs even had that much money but decided to take the chance and fill the order.

The two drug lords agreed to have Killa Fred and Body Bag deliver the money to Castilino in Juarez, then in turn would follow 18 wheelers into El Paso, Texas. From there they would unload the bricks to an awaiting vehicle and then drive back to the Chi. Killa Fred and Body Bag pulled up to Castilino's estate in a rented F-150.

"You see the truck?" Killa Fred asked noticing the semi parked to the side.

"Yea. That boy loaded with candy too." Body Bag replied ready to make the biggest score of his life.

"Just remember, Bag. Stick to the script and this gone be like taking candy from a baby." Killa Fred parked behind a blue Phantom Rolls Royce.

Castilino stood in the driveway smoking a cigar filled with Mexico's finest.

"Como estas, amigo," Castilino greeted as Killa Fred and Body Bag got out the truck.

Killa Fred grabbed two leather briefcases from the back of the truck bed. Two bodyguards stood next to Castilino clutching MPS machine guns. "Como estas to you my friend. Nice to see you again, El-Senor," Killa Fred greeted, shaking hands with the drug boss. This was his second time meeting Castilino.

"You come bearing gifts?" Castilino nodded to the briefcases.

"Like they say. No money like dope money." Killa Fed replied in a serious demeanor.

"You speak the truth, mijo."

At that moment the two security men came over to pat Killa Fred and Body Bag down. Body Bag tensed up. he hated being touched by niggas. A mean mug plastered his face.

"Don't worry, my friend, this is just protocol. Not personal." Castilino said noticing Body Bag's defensive character.

The two were led inside the exclusive mansion. Castilino had the $10-million-dollar home built from the ground from all blood money. Castilino led them to a study room overlooking the City of

Juarez. Taking a seat behind a large oak desk Castilino offered the two men a seat. Killa Fred and Body Bag took a seat on large sectional sofa as one of the bodyguards posted and the other one stood on security outside of the door.

"Now shall we get down to business my friends? My time is valuable, and as you Americans say, time is money." Castilino said relighting his blunt. After taking a pull he extended the weed to Body Bag. "No?"

"Na, I'm cool fam. Don't mix business with pleasure."

Castilino was slightly offended but didn't let it show.

Killa Fred cleared his throat before he spoke. "Mr. Biggs sends his love and respect as always, but he sends a message."

"And what's that?"

"For starters he's not feeling how we was on hold for all that time. We spend millions with you constantly and feel we should have a stronger business relationship than that. Secondly, if we are spending 40 mill with you on this shipment out of courtesy, you should give us a lower number, being that we have extensive history."

Castilino hit the weed and blew smoke through his nostrils. "Why didn't Mr. Biggs discuss this with me?" The Bodyguard tightened his chubby fingers on the MPS.

"I guess he figured more words didn't need to be explained."

"Oh, I see. So, you come here trying to throw a monkey wrench in the game." Castilino put the blunt out in the marble ashtray. In an icy tone he said, "My prices remain the same."

"I figured you would say that." Killa Fred stood with the two briefcases and placed them flat on Castilino's desk.

Castilino watched him menacingly while Killa Fred put in the combination on the lock mechanism and opened the briefcase. What Castilino thought was 40-million in drug money was nothing but guns. Killa Fred retrieved the silenced .45 Colt with the quickness, turned to the bodyguard and squeezed the trigger. *Pssst!* The hydro shock penetrated his skull blowing his brains on the wall. His body fell to the floor without life. Now Castilino sat with the same murder weapon pointed in his face.

"You make a sound and you gone be next, chico." Killa Fred threatened through clenched teeth.

Castilino remained in Boss mode. "You're making a big mistake my friend."

"Shut the fuck up. Where the keys to the truck?" Body Bag grabbed the Mac 10 from the suitcase.

Castilino took the keys from his pocket that he was supposed to give the driver and laid them on the table. "I piss a 1,000 kilos," Castilino hissed.

"Get your ss up." Killa Fred grabbed the back of his shirt forcing him to his feet while Body Bag hid on the side of the door with the Mac. "Now. In English, I want you to call the other guard in here."

"You will not get away with this." Killa Fred slapped him with the pistol, splitting the back of his head like Moses split the Red Sea. Blood spilled onto the floor. "Hector, come in here!" Castilino wiped the blood from his face, now seeing the danger of his situation. And his life.

The door opened and Hector stepped in. Seeing his boss in a bloody mess made him raise his weapon. Body Bag put the silenced Mac 10 to the back of his head and squeezed. The sound was like a car door being slammed as Hector's brain tissue and skull fragments sprayed from his cranium, his body dropping to the floor.

"Now we gone walk out of here nice and slow. You follow directions, you live. And you disobey, you die. Comprende?"

Castilino nodded his head in understanding. Killa Fed and Body Bag led Castilino out the front door of the mansion at gunpoint. There, guards stood posted. Wasting no time and taking no chance, Body Bag let the Mac 10 spit venom, spraying the guards down with hilarious automatic gunfire.

"Body Bag, grab the truck." Killa Fred said tossing him the keys to the 18 wheeler.

Body Bag walked up to Castilino who bled profusely and said. "On them high ass prices. No comprende," then got him twice in the stomach.

Castilino fell to the pavement, laying in a puddle of his own blood.

Body Bag hopped in the semi as Killa Fred jumped in the F-150. The two gangsters left the Cartel Boss for dead. They bounced with 6,000 kilos of uncut heroin, on their way back to the Chi.

Mr. Biggs and the Body Snatchers reigned supreme and dominated the dope game in the Midwest. Mr. Biggs was crowned King of Chicago's underworld and the road to riches was poured in gold. Everything was casual for Mr. Biggs until he received a disturbing phone call.

"Hello," he answered.

"You missed, Pi-dogo. Coward." Mr. Biggs knew who the voice belonged to. "I will not sleep until I have your head on a platter!" Castilino sneered into the receiver before he left Mr. Biggs with the did tone. They thought he was resting in peace, but the boss of the Medina Cartel was very much alive.

Body Bag was brought back to reality when a Red Bentley Truck pulled into the driveway of the house. The 28-inch Giovani's had the truck siting up like a monster as the 15-inch flat screen hanging from the ceiling of the whip was visible. Body Bag watched as Ronnie and a female exited the SUV. The diamond-studded Breitling on his wrist read 4:30 am. After watching Ronnie and the chick enter the crib, Body Bag pulled the black ski mask over his face and put his hands on a new pair of Nike gloves. Checking the 100-round drum on the assault rifle he got out the car.

Ronnie plopped down on the sectional sofa and turned on the 55-inch plasma TV that decorated his wall. He had just come from the club. Popping bottles of Rosè, he ran into a local hood rat by the name of Fay. the Kush in Ronnie's system along with a half a gram of Molly he consumed had him ready to tear a lining out of Fay's pussy. Ronnie proceeded to roll another blunt of Sticky.

"Shorty, you over there sitting on the couch like you shy or something. Let a nigga feel what that mouth like." Ronnie said putting the finishing touches on the blunt.

Fay got up and stepped to her business. She knew Ronnie was a baller and if she played her cards right, she would be getting all of his cash. She was the true definition of a gold digger. Kneeling between his legs she unzipped his Tru Religion's and freed his 10 inch monster from the confines of his boxer briefs and engulfed as much of him as she could. The warmth of Fay's mouth caused Ronnie to moan in ecstasy while he lit the blunt and inhaled. Ronnie was enjoying Fay's head game until he heard a loud crashing noise, as his door was being kicked in. Fay jumped back in horror at the sight of the masked gunmen pointing a Choppa in their direction. She let out a piercing scream. Body Bag wasted no time and squeezed the trigger, putting two 223's in her face, spraying her brains and weave on Ronnie's bare chest. The spent shell cases littered the floor.

"You can have whatever you want. Please don't shoot me. I got like 30 bands in my room. It's yours. Please." Ronnie pleaded to the masked man. Body Bag pulled off the ski mask. At that moment Ronnie knew his young life was over. "I'm sorry, bro." Ronnie never got a chance to finish his sentence.

Body Bag stood over him with the rifle and put 60 rounds into his face, head and chest. The loud barking from the rifle awoke the entire block. Seeing that his work was official Body Bag fled from the house, leaving a smell of death and gun smoke. He had missed one hit, and vowed he had to finish it. He had to find Lil' Tony, ASAP.

Chapter 9

Malaki was at Poncho's apartment in the Northside, politicking the death of Mr. Biggs. On the way to Poncho's crib, Poncho told Malaki about his infatuation with murdering the gang chief. He added that he held a death list pertaining to the gang's infrastructure. Poncho explained that the Body Snatcher organization was a dangerous that he held a death list pertaining Mr. Biggs infrastructure at the MOB, including workers, security and money makers by name, location and other detrimental information that would lead to the fall off the Body Snatchers.

Malaki sat on Poncho's sectional sofa. In his hands was the death list. Malaki looked over the names in the Murda Book. "Why haven't you already eliminated these individuals?" Malaki questioned.

Poncho sat on the couch, loading a clip into an automatic weapon. "My friend, I could've killed them over and over again. But why? I was sent to kill Mr. Biggs, not the entire organization."

Malaki looked up from the Murda Book. "So why show me this book?"

"I show you the book because you told me you want war with these people, so I'm giving you an advantage, amigo."

Malaki nodded his head in understanding, closing the book. "What do I owe you for this information that you have given? Nothing in life is for free. Everything has a price." Malaki's voice dripped venom as the thought of violence invaded his thoughts.

Poncho held up his hands in peace. "Listen, my friend, I agree with you. Nothing in life is free. Everything has a price tag in this life that we live. All I ask is that you let me assist you in your quest to murder these men. Let's remember, I have a contract to fill as well, and I feel two heads are always better than one." Poncho reminded him. They had the same target in their crosshairs. He could easily let Malaki knock Mr. Biggs off. It would cause him a lot of trouble, but he wanted in on the bloodshed and would have it no other way.

Malaki stood up. "How do I know that I can trust you? Not even an hour ago you had a gun to the back of my head."

"It's not about trust, my friend. If you continue without me and my help you will surely fail. You will be dead by the end of the month, I'm sure. I could have easily killed you, I had your Glock, my friend. I want nothing more than to see you succeed in your endeavors. But, even more, it is a must Mr. Biggs dies. Do you agree?"

Malaki thought long and hard. Without Poncho and the death list he would never be able to get close to Mr. Biggs. he didn't even have a clue. Poncho was right. If he wanted to kill Malaki, he surely held his life in his hands. He could've shot him dead and his mission would've been over before it even started. Malaki thought back to what Commander Sanchez preached to him about the importance of allies.

"My son. Always remember in war you are only as strong as your allies. Without allies in war, my son, you are and will remain a still target."

At that point, Malaki made up his mind to let Poncho accompany him in his revenge. Malaki extended his hand to the Mexican assassin.

Poncho smiled, accepting his hand. "I will not let you down, my friend."

"If you betray me in anyway, I will kill you." Malaki meant every word that he spoke.

Poncho shook his head. "You need to loosen up, my friend. Save the aggression for the battlefield."

Malaki ignored his remark. "Do you know where I can get some guns?"

"Follow me, amigo."

Malaki followed Poncho to his bedroom. Kneeling, Poncho reached under his bed pulling a large plastic case from under it. Malaki looked on in anticipation. Poncho opened the large case. What Malaki saw made a chill go through his spine. Inside the case sat 8 different semi-automatic handguns at different calibers, four short barrel assault rifles, and two clay boxes that from his experience, he knew to be C-4. Poncho grabbed a . 223 Bushmaster and passed it to Malaki. He admired the American made weapon.

While Malaki was toying with the gun, Poncho walked inside his walk-in closet and returned holding two long rifles and laid them on the bed. "Have you ever been haunting, my friend?" Poncho said with an evil smirk on his face.

Malaki looked at the powerful 30 aught 6 Bolt action rifle and 50 caliber bear that laid next to it. With the size of the ferocious weapons Malaki could envision Mr. Biggs being plastered on the concrete. "My father was the best sniper in the country before he was killed. His blood runs through my veins." Malaki returned picking up the 30 and 6.

"Well, my friend, we make no progress sitting here. I say we hit the streets."

"Where do we start?"

"The say when you mess with a man's money you bring him out of character."

"What do you mean?"

Poncho grabbed the black Murder Book. "Listen, amigo. This is how we will bring Mr. Biggs and his empire to their knees." Poncho and Malaki sat in the apartment, plotting and scheming. They were about to bring an evilness to the city of Chicago that had not been seen since the days of Al Capone.

Homicide Detective Michael Colhoun had retired 18 years ago after the Chicago Police Department had killed Byron Hobson in a standoff on the city's westside. Throughout his career Colhoun had seen it all in the murderous street of Chicago. After spending 20 years on the force, he had become accustomed to violence. His main objective was to clean up the streets, so he was his job. He hated gang members and drug dealers all the same with disgust. Billy Good and the Mafias were his main targets. Putting the gang chief away in a United State Penitentiary had become a decision for him, so when Billy Good was sentenced to 360 months hard time, Calhoun was relieved. Calhoun's celebration of victory was short lived when another up and coming goon stood up to take Billy Good's place, leading the Mafia in his own politics. Byron Hobson. After eliminating his rivals in a hell of blood and shell casings, with experience in the military, Calhoun was met with a new challenge that he took head on. After relieving Byron of his young life, the tale of the streets had taken its last course on him. Calhoun was happily married to his high school sweetheart. Valie. They had beautiful twin daughters who were both enrolled in the University of Illinois studying law. The violence that the streets unleashed was knocking on Calhoun's door, and he felt it was the perfect time to make his escape to the happily ever after ending. He would have to if he ever wanted to see his beautiful daughters walk across the stage and pursue their dreams.

Colhoun folded the Chicago Tribune newspaper and placed it on the table. He had just read the local section of the paper. The murder count had just reached 750 and the year was far from over. He shook his head in disgust. The victims were mostly kids, with ages ranging from 13 to 21. The United States had just elected a new president— a Republican who cared less about the lives of Chicagoans. The country was in an uproar. At a time like this Colhoun silently wished that he would've never retired from the police force. Maybe he would have done something to make a difference in the streets. Just maybe.

Valie emerged from the kitchen with two glasses of ice-tea. She handed one to her husband. Valie took a seat next to him. "What's in the paper, honey?" She asked taking a sip from her tea.

"Murder and mayhem, sweetie." He replied taking a sip.

"It seems like it worries you."

"I just think that every time an officer punches that clock they don't want to make a difference. I mean, every time they hit these streets it's a chance they might not make it home to their family."

"You just don't know how many nights I stayed up waiting for you. Praying and hoping that you would walk through that door." Valie recounted the long, worry-filled nights she went through while Calhoun was on the frontline for two decades.

"Yeah, I know, honey. It's just messed up out there and I wish I could do something. You know? Then you have this sucker president who has his priorities messed up and making the world a worse place."

"I agree, baby," Valie replied downing the rest of her tea. She hated speaking politics with her husband, but being a loyal wife, she was always there for him when he needed to vent. Standing up she placed a warm kiss on his check, taking his empty glass. She said, "Don't worry, baby. Everything will be planned, and everything will work itself out. God has a plan for us all. let's just be thankful for our health and safety." Valie headed to the kitchen, leaving her husband in his thoughts.

He had a lot to be thankful for. He had a beautiful wife and two brilliant children. Life was good and he had escaped the grave city streets in the Chi.

S. Allen

Chapter 10

Tobias stood at the Kenmore stove watching the cocaine bubble up inside the Pyrex. He was in a dingy wife beater, black Dickie pants and Nike Air-Max boots with a chrome Taurus 9-millimeter fitting snug on his waistline. He had been in the trap all day cooking up cocaine along with his squad, Derrick, Fatman and Manny. Mr. Biggs not only flooded the streets with potent heroin, but with the best cocaine in the Midwest. He had his hands in everything involving the drug game, and the trap on 78th and Heritage was just a piece of his conglomerate.

Tobias watched the cocaine melt into an oily substance before he added some Arm & Hammer baking soda. Smoking on a blunt filled with Sour Diesel Kush Tobias grabbed the Pyrex off the stove. The steam coming from the pot looked like a misty fog. Walking to the sink he turned on the cold water. After applying a small amount of the water in the pot, the coolness of the H20 gave the cocaine a chemical reaction, causing it to form into a mushy substance. Tobias took a spoon and began to whip the drugs, add a little more baking soda and water, and the cocaine began to harden. After he completed the process, what was once powder cocaine was now crack. He removed the crack from the pot and placed it on a large plate. This was the last of the coke that need to be cooked. They had already cooked 3 kilos.

"Butter, my nigga." Tobias said admiring the perfectly cooked drugs.

Fatman stood on the side by the sink, putting Kush in a split blunt. "You think you like that, huh?"

"You already know I'm a beast. Look at that cookie on that plate." Tobias took a short pull from the weed, blowing smoke through his nostrils before he sat on the table and picked up a razor to cut the crack up.

Fatman put the finishing touches on his blunt and then dried it with a lighter. "I keep telling y'all. We wasting our time with this stove shit. We could've dry cooked this shit with ammonia and finished with these bricks." Fatman lit the blunt and inhaled deeply.

"The hypes don't like it like that bruh, and pulse too much of it will bust their heart. We don't need a bunch of clucks falling out dead over here. If that happens, the Feds gone get on us with the quickness. Straight up!" Tobias said putting a blunt out in the ashtray. "Aye. Derrick. Manny! Come on, my niggas, so we can bag up this last half of a brick." Tobias yelled to his potnas that were in the living room engaged in a game of NBA 2K on a huge flat screen TV.

"Man, I had the nigga down 20 points." Manny started walking in the kitchen, taking a seat at the kitchen table.

Derrick fell in, pulling up hips sagging Givenchy jeans. "Quit stunting, I was about to come back on that ass. You knew what it is." Derrick grabbed the blunt from Fatman.

The four friends called themselves the Coke Boys, and grew with each other from the sandbox. They were getting money slinging stones on Heritage but never had a consistent plug so that they could advance in the crack game. Mr. Biggs, after hearing about the drug block, sent his cronies to take it over. With a killer click like the Body Snatchers, the Coke Boys had no choice but to oblige. It was either get down or lay down, and the Coke Boys decided it was in their best interest to get down. Ever since then the thugs had been getting money with the Body Snatchers. Taking care of the duties, cooking, bagging and distributing the work tonight was just another night in the trap.

"Tell me again why we are sitting here in the car instead of going in there asking for Mr. Biggs?" Malaki asked from the passenger seat of the tinted Ford Taurus parked on 78th and Hermitage.

Poncho sat behind the wheel dressed in all black with a large hunting knife resting on his lap. They had been watching the house all night. Tobia's and the Coke Boys were on the death list. Poncho knew that the spot on Hermitage was bringing Mr. Biggs an easterly amount of cash. Through surveillance he knew the Coke Boys were pumping a lot of work on the block because the amount of drug traffic. He knew at 12:30 at night an individual would come and pick up the money. Looking at his army fatigue G-Shock watch Poncho saw that it was 11:45. "I told you, my friend, we are going to take all the money that they made today. You know? Put a dent in Mr. Briggs' pockets and then we will take their lives. Comprende?"

Malaki continued looking out the window toward the house they were about to invade. He was anxious to get this over and done with. Screwing the silencer on his Glock, Malaki pulled the slide back to chamber a hollow point round. "Instead of us waiting in the car all night, why not just go in there?"

"My friend. You must learn to have patience. Patience is always a virtue, always remember that. Why run to the cow when we can have the cow ran to us?" Poncho dropped a jewel on Malaki.

Malaki was trained well but Poncho had the experience in the battlefield that Malaki didn't. "I guess."

Fifteen minutes later the Coke Boys were still hard at work bagging up the drugs.

"Is it some more sandwich bags over there?" Manny asked slicing a large piece of crack with the razor. An empty box was in the middle of the table.

"Damn. That's the last of the baggies, Joe." Derrick said after he searched the cabinets coming up blank.

Tobias continued to slice up the rocks. "One of y'all go to the corner store right quick so we can finish this shit and get it over with and get up outta here." Derrick and Manny looked at each other. Neither wanted to make the trip to the store. Tobias looked back at them. "Man, can one of y'all please hurry the fuck up!" Tobias was getting agitated and wanted to finish what they were doing.

Derrick, already having the keys to the Cadillac DTS in his pocket, knew he would be the one to make the run.

"I'll be right back fam." Derrick walked out the house.

Tobias and Manny erupted in laughter.

"Look, Malaki." Poncho said as he watched Derrick hop in the Lac.

"Where is he going?" Malaki asked with his hand tight on his gun.

"I don't know, amigo. I have a feeling he's coming back real soon. When he does, we will be ready to make our move."

Malaki nodded his head. The two assassins exited the car and made their way across the street.

A few minutes later Derrick was parking the whip in front of the trap. After turning the ignition off he stayed in the car talking on his cell phone to a chick named ReeRee. He had been trying to sex ReeRee for the past week and was finally breaking down the walls to get her in his bed. "Alright, shorty, I'ma call you when I leave the block." She replied by saying something freaky before she hung up the phone. Derrick hopped out the vehicle carrying a brown paper bag containing the sandwich bags and blunts. When he approached the front door, he was about to give the coded knock until he felt something hard and cold being pressed against his skull. The brown bag fell to the floor.

"Shhhh. My friend. How many in the house?"

"Who are you?" Derrick asked as he passed gas, visibly spooked.

Poncho pressed the gun harder against his cranium. "I only ask one more time. Then I put your brains on the ground and find out myself." Poncho's tone was demon-like.

"It's two fam. Why don't you let me go? I told you what you wanted to know. Please don't shoot me."

Derrick pleaded. Poncho shook his head at the disloyalty of this foot soldier. "I'll let you go after you get us in the house. You have my word."

Malaki stood to the side, a black ski mask covered his face making him look like a ninja. Derrick knocked on the door 6 times.

"It's about time this nigga got back." Manny stood from the table hearing the coded knock at the door. After taking the chain off the door and undoing the dead bolts he opened it. The only thing he saw was a quick bright flash and then he was sent to eternal darkness. He was shot in the face at point blank range. The silenced Glock 10-millimeter jerked once in Malaki's hand, the spent shell casing flew from the weapon.

Walking into the house, Malaki kept his Glock extended in front of him. Poncho held Derrick by his collar with his gun to his rib cage, walking him into the kitchen, identity concealed. Tobias and

Manny were busy with the task at hand until Malaki fired a 10-millimeter round at the table causing both men to quickly look up.

"What the fuck!" He reached for the 40 that laid on the table but was a millisecond late.

Malaki sent a silent hot slug that hit Fatman in his throat. Fatman grabbed at his throat as he grasped for air while blood leaked through his fingers. His attempt to live was futile. Falling out of the chair, he escaped into the afterlife.

"What's good, fam? Y'all can take the money and the drugs. It's under the kitchen sink." Tobias said holding his hands up. Malaki raised the hot Glock. "Nooooo!" Tobias' screams fell on deaf ears. The Glock jerked twice. Tobias' brains splattered on the wall behind him.

Derrick pissed his pants. "You said you were going to let me go. Please. I didn't see anything. I promise y'all."

Malaki went to the sink and looked under it. Two Nike gym bags sat there. After unzipping the bags, dead presidents stared him in his face. Malaki nodded his head at Pocho who put this handgun in its holster and grabbed the hunting knife from the sheath that was on his waist.

Derrick looked at the knife in horror. "I thought you were going to let me go?"

"I am going to let you go, my friend. I'm going to let you go and meet your creator." Poncho sneered before he sank the knife into Derrick's stomach. Derrick felt the cold stainless steel enter his belly. Poncho used the knife like a saw; the jagged edges on the knife cut Derrick like butter. After retrieving the blade from Derrick's abdomen his body hit the floor with a loud thud as he bled out. The smell of shit and copper rose from his corpse. Poncho wiped the bloody murder weapon on Derrick's shirt before sticking it back in its sheath. "Let's go, Eśe," Poncho said behind his mask.

Grabbing the bags full of cash Malaki followed him out the house. After jumping in the car, they pulled off into the darkness. War had just been declared on the Body Snatchers and it was a war that was far from over.

S. Allen

Chapter 11

Deuce Dilla pushed the cherry red Corvette 60 miles per hour down I-95 coming from St. Louis. It was 1:00 in the morning. He had just dropped off a few kilos of heroin for Killa Fred. At the end of every month Deuce would make the trip to the low. He had been making the trip for the last two years. At only 21 Deuce was addicted to the fast life that the Body Snatchers provided for him. He was in a hurry to get back to the Chi, it was still early and if he made it back in time, he would still be able to hit the club up. Deuce's thoughts were invaded when he saw the red and blue lights in his rearview mirror.

"Fuck!" He cussed out loud thinking about the quarter million dollars and pistol that he had on the backseat. Pulling the expensive whip over he looked in the rearview mirror and saw two officers exit the unmarked Crown Victoria.

One of the officers knocked on his window signaling him to roll the window down. His hands resting on his holstered Glock.

Doing as he was told, Deuce lowered the tinted window. "What's the problem, officer?" Beads of sweat were visible on his forehead.

"Drivers license and registration, sir." The officer had shades covering his eyes. The other stood on the other side of the car; hand on his weapon.

"Why you pulling me over?" Deuce Dillion asked handing the officer his credentials.

The officer ignored him, analyzing the license. "Step out of the car."

"For what?" Deuce Dillon was nervous as shit when the officer pulled the Glock from his holster.

"I'm not going to ask you again. Get out of the car slowly."

Deuce Dillion did as he was told, shaking his head in disbelief. Once out the car he was ordered to place his hands on the hood of the car.

"Spread 'em." The officer commanded as he proceeded to pat him down. Retrieving a pair of handcuffs from his belt the officer slapped them on Deuce Dillon's wrist. The officer nodded to his partner, who stood silently on the other side of the vehicle. The officer began to search the car.

Deuce Dillon was now starting to sweat profusely as he watched the officer grab the bags from the backseat and place it on the hood of the Vette. "What's in the bag?" The officer asked. Deuce Dillon remained silent. The officer unzipped the duffel bags. "Looks like we have it the jackpot." The officer replied.

"Looks like we have a weapon also." The officer with Deuce smirked.

"It's not mine." Deuce lied.

"Don't worry, my friend. You not go to jail. You going to hell."

Pop! Poncho shot Deuce Dillon in the head. He fell back into the Corvette. Putting the rest of his body in the car, Poncho closed the door with his gloved hand and grabbed the bags of blood money leaving Deuce Dillan lifeless inside the whip. Malaki sat in passenger side of the car with the black bag in his hands. Taking a pen from his front pocket he crossed off the name of the man they had just executed.

***

Mr. Biggs sat in the backseat of his Maybach, riding through downtown Chicago. He had just pushed end on his iPhone. Killa Fed had just informed him about the Murders of the Coke Boys in the trap house on 71st and Hermitage. He also told him about Deuce's body getting found on the inside of his car. Mr. Biggs wasn't stressed, he could care less about the lives of the young men killed. In his mind he felt that in the dope game he was sure of two things. Either riches or death. The soldier could be replaced. His worry was the money he lost in the process. He was confused. He didn't know if the killings were connected, or if they were isolated incidents. If they were connected that meant he had some enemies on his line. Mr. Biggs told Killa Fred to tighten up and keep his eyes open. He had been at the top for almost two decades and would be damned if he let the crown fall from his head.

"Walter, make a left at the next light and pull into that parking lot." Mr. Biggs told his driver. A few moments later the Maybach pulled into a lot along the side of a Cadillac Escalade. Getting out of the car Mr. Biggs got into the backseat of the truck. The smell of high grade Marijuana hit him in the face.

An older African man draped in diamonds held a large cigar filled with weed, his eyes bloodshot red. "You are late, Mr. Boi." The African said taking a long pull of the weed.

"My apologies, Rasta. I had some important business to tend to."

"You have problems in your organization?"

Mr. Biggs stroked his grey goatee. "Nothing I can't take care of."

"Good. I would hate to stop what we have going on."

"Not at all. Are we still on schedule for the next shipment?" Mr. Biggs asked accepting the weed from Rasta.

"As always, Mr. Boi. Nothing has changed. When will I receive my money?"

Mr. Biggs blew a thick cloud of smoke before he spoke. "Your money is already in your account as of this morning."

Rasta smiled. "Biggs, you keep on doing what you are doing you will be a very wealthy man." Rasta received the weed back from Mr. Biggs.

"That's the plan." Mr. Biggs was on the road to riches. His weight was all the way up, and dropping $10-million on the plug for re-up was living proof. The lust for power was evident in his heart, but if he wanted to remain king, he knew he had to tighten up and stay focused on his goals.

It had been a couple days since the murders of the Coke Boys and Deuce Dillon. Malaki and Poncho had been putting in work since they met. They had eliminated a few names in the Murder Book but it was far from over. The two killers were at a Red Lobster restaurant discussing murder. They were comfortable. The drugs and money they confiscated from the hits were put in a safe place that they only knew of the whereabouts. Poncho told Malaki it would come in handy later on. Malaki could care less about the money or drugs; his only concern was the death of Mr. Biggs. Taken a bite of his shrimp Malaki heard a slight commotion in the next booth. The other booth was occupied by an exotic looking female and a dark skinned male who seemed to be agitated or angry.

"So, I was thinking, my friend. On the list is a Eśe by the name of Max G. He is supposed to be moving a lot of high-grade Mota for Mr. Biggs in some housing projects called the Robert Taylors." Poncho said tearing into his lobster.

"When you want to do it?" Malaki asked cutting his eye at the beautiful woman in the next booth. Her looks were intoxicating him as her rude boyfriend was aggravating him with the way he was speaking to her. Malaki tried to block her from his mind and focus on Poncho and what he was saying.

"I don't know, Eśe. Those projects are very dangerous, they have security out there all of the time. They have a strategic operation going on. They are called the Gangster's. They all work for Mr. Biggs. We have to find a way to get in there. Take care of our business and get out without incident if we want to live." Said Poncho.

Malaki let what Poncho said marinate his mind. His concentration was broken when he heard the guy in the next booth call the woman a bitch. After wiping his mouth with a napkin Malaki politely excused himself from the table. "Excuse me."

"Where you going, Eśe?"

Malaki walked over to the booth and stood there with his hands behind his back.

The disrespectful dude looked up at him. "What the fuck you want?" The guy asked with a mean mug on his face.

"For you to leave the woman alone." Malaki said nonchalantly.

"Man, fuck off. This my bitch." The guy replied and tried to stand to his feet.

Malaki effortlessly pushed him back down in the booth. The female sat in silence while the guy attempted to stand back up. This time Malaki chopped him in the throat. The guy grabbed his neck as he lost his breath. Grabbing his hand, Malaki twisted his wrist until he heard a snapping sound, breaking it. Still holding his wrist Malaki pulled the guy close and whispered in his ear through clenched teeth, "Leave the woman or I will pull your heart through your chest and make you swallow it. Do I make myself clear?"

"Yes. Yes." The guy started before Malaki pushed him from the table. The terrified bully fell, trying to get way, tripping over his own feet making a dash for the door.

Malaki took a seat in the booth with the exotic looking female who had her mouth open in shock. "Are you alright?" He asked her. The woman nodded. "What's your name?"

"My name is Nicki," she managed to say. Malaki smiled as he wiped a tear that fell from her cheek. "Thank you." Nicki said loving the warm feeling from Malaki's hand.

"No problem. My name is Malaki. I didn't mean to interfere in you and your man's business. It's just you are too pretty to be talked to like that. I couldn't just sit there and let him disrespect you."

Malaki's word melted her heart. She let a smile come across her face. "He's not really my boyfriend; we've only been seeing each other for a month, but it's over now." Now mad at herself for wasting her time on a lame in the first place, there was an awkward silence until Malaki broke it.

"Listen. I was wondering if maybe I can get your phone number?" He was nervous when he spoke, he wasn't used to asking women out. He was like a trained robot. Trained for combat. And serving death.

Nicki picked up on his shyness and loved every minute of it. She loved his serious goon demeanor and found it sexy. Without saying a word she pulled out a pen from her Gucci handbag, wrote her a number on a napkin and slid it across the table to Malaki.

Malaki looked at the number and locked it into his mental. "When call I call you?"

"Whenever you think about me." She replied softly before she stood to leave.

Walking off Malaki watched as her voluptuous ass cheeks bounced with each step. He definitely had to find out more about Ms. Nicki and soon.

Sitting in the booth with Poncho, Poncho started shaking his head. "You do know they call that Captain Save a Hoe. Don't you?" Poncho joked.

Malaki ignored Poncho's remarks. He didn't understand what it meant anyway. The two assassins finished their meals all the while plotting how they were going to kill Max G. They were now in the battlefield, and shit was about to get real, real quick.

Chapter 12

Malaki laid on the king size bed inside his hotel suite. In his hand he held is cell phone debating on if he should call Commander Sanchez. He told himself he wasn't going to call his mentor until he had completed his mission. Staring at his phone he decided to call his father and let him know what was going on. So much had happened since he landed in Chicago. Before entering the blood-soaked city, he had never committed murder. Only trained for it. Malaki had already caught 7 bodies. The killing didn't bother him. He was driven by a stronger force. The revenge of his parent's death was his ambition.

He missed Commander Sanchez dearly. His presence as well as his words of wisdom. Malaki dialed his number. It rang three times before he heard the comforting voice of his mentor.

"Hello?"

"It's me, papa." Malaki responded.

"Malaki, my son. How are you?"

"I'm fine, Papa, and you?"

"I'm doing well. How are you and what is your status?" Commander Sanchez probed, wanting to know if Malaki was proceeding in his endeavor. The sooner he handled his functions, the sooner he would return home.

"I'm getting close, papa. I have met somebody. Somebody who shares my same goals and ambitions."

Commander Sanchez listened intently to his son.

"Papa, I will not rest until—"

Commander Sanchez cut him off. "Be smart in your decisions and move with your first instincts, because it will save your life. Always remember, trust must be earned." Commander Sanchez schooled.

Malaki understood his father completely. Malaki trusted Pocho so far. Without Poncho, Malaki would be lost without a clue and possibly dead.

"I have some information for you. You remember the detective we spoke of in your father's murder?"

"Yes, papa."

"I have come across his file. Look for it in the mail in the next two weeks." Commander said. He had gotten the information on the detective long ago. He held it form Malaki for a reason. He knew that it was a lot of heat when dealing with the murder of a cop, and he wanted Malaki to be mentally ready. He would send the information to his son to the secret PO Box that Malaki had attained.

Malaki's blood pumped through his veins rapidly from receiving the information Commander Sanchez had just given him. He waited for years to obtain it. In a matter of hours, he would have the info he needed to kill the person responsible for the death of his father. "I will be waiting for it, papa. I will not fail."

"I know, son. You are in my prayers. Hurry with your mission so you can get back home."

"I love you, papa."

"I love you too."

Malaki ended the call. His anticipation was growing by the minute. Malaki laid on his back and let his mind drift into the thought of murder.

***

Nicki swerved in and out of the midday traffic in her BMW. She had just gotten off work, pulling a 9-hour shift at the O'Hare Airport. At 29 years old she was single, independent and beautiful. Nicki owned a small home in Harvey, Illinois right outside of Cook County. With her hectic work schedule, it was hard for her to date. Time did not permit it. She had been seeing Ricky for the last month. Ricky worked at the airport with her and was always flirting with her. He was funny, always made her laugh, and with his dark, smooth skin, Nicki found him attractive.

After 6 months of constant flirting Nicki decided to give Ricky a chance. Not the one to give her goodies away right away, Nicki wanted to get to know Ricky better before she invited him into her bed. Ricky was begging to get acquainted, waiting for the pussy and becoming aggressive. That's what the argument at the restaurant was about. Him getting some nookie. Nicki decided to end their short-lived relationship right then. Ricky wasn't feeling his dismissal and reacted by cursing her out, calling her everything except a child of God. Nicki had never been so embarrassed in her life. That was until her knight and shining armor came to her rescue. He was caring as she felt protection when in his presence. she couldn't keep her mind off him. His caramel complexion, low haircut and crispy goatee was sexy, not to mention his wide shoulders. She could tell he spent countless hours in the gym. Nicki found his words sincere and his actions sealed the deal. She had given him the number and he still hadn't called. Every time her phone rang she prayed it was Malaki, but was disappointed each time.

Nicki made it home a little after 6:00 in the evening. Walking in the house she took off her Jimmy-Choo heels and placed them in the closet. Her feet ached something terrible. The whole shift she stood on her feet yearning to come home and soak in a bubble bath. Nicki went upstairs and ran herself a hot bubble bath, pouring some Bath and Body raspberry scented fragrance in the tub. Going to the kitchen she went to the refrigerator and grabbed the half bottle of Moscato and went back upstairs. After unbuttoning her shirt Nicki removed her Victoria's Secret lace bra. Her double D's sparing loose. Pulling her matching thongs off Nicki put her long, silky hair into a bun and stepped into the tub. The water was hot just like she liked it.

After easing her thick frame into the water she grabbed the bottle of Moscato and took a sip. Her cell phone sat at the base of the tub. Sinking down into the water Nicki started to feel relaxed after a hard day at work. The Moscato had her feeling a little tipsy. She started to visualize Malaki. She was so attracted to him. It had been awhile since she had been with a man. Her hand slid down to her fat vagina. Nicki inserted one of her fingers into her tight love box. And then two. Biting her bottom lip, she started to finger herself. Her eyes closed as he imagined Malaki using his tongue on it, pleasuring her, bringing her into a climax. Popping her clit Nicki felt her button swell up. On the verge of cumming, her cell phone interrupted her freak session. "Damn," she cursed to herself, mad that she didn't get her nut off. "Hello?" she answered with a slight attitude.

"Uhm, may I speak to Nicki?" The caller asked.

Nicki instantly knew who the voice belonged to. "Malaki?" Nicki was embarrassed that Malaki called while she was masturbating, thinking about him.

"How are you? I figured I would give you a call and see how you are doing."

"Actually, I was waiting for your call." Nicki said shyly.

"I was wondering if I could take you out. Get to know you a little better."

"I don't know, Malaki, you seem kind of dangerous." Nicki said in a sexy tone.

Malaki loved her voice. He didn't know how to respond.

"Boy, I'm just playing with you. I would love to go out with you. It's the least I can do for you coming to my rescue."

"Nicki, that was just the right thing to do."

"I guess." Nicki and Malaki talked on the phone for hours getting to know each other, making plans to see each other on Friday night.

After talking with Malaki, Nicki got out the tub which was now lukewarm. She was on Cloud 9 and couldn't wait to see her knight in shining armor.

Malaki hung up. He was happy that Nicki had agreed to go out to dinner with him on Friday. The reason he hadn't called was because he was nervous. He was drawn to Nicki the first time he set his eyes on her. Malaki tossed his phone on the bed and walked over to the window. His suite was on the 21st floor. From his view, he could see the whole city of Chicago.

It was dark outside as he watched the hustle and bustle of the city. It was his first time in a major city. He couldn't seem to understand how such a beautiful city could be so dangerous, claiming the lives of so many young black males. The gang activity in Chicago was in and it was all motivated by drugs. The young thugs in the ghetto of the Chi were infatuated with the riches that the drug game brought, and willing to kill for their territories. Malaki shook his head. Who was he to pass judgment? He had contributed to the high murder rate in the city of Chi. He was no different than the thugs that ran the streets, murdering without conscious, leaving families to mourn. Leaving children without fathers.

The thought of his own parents brought him back to reality. Malaki pulled a piece of paper from his Prada jogging pants and read the information again. He had read it over 100 times already. Commander Sanchez had sent it to his PO Box a few days ago. Malaki put the paper back in his pocket. He would take care of the situation soon. Very soon. But right now, he and Poncho had something to take care of. It was time to get active. Grabbing his phone Malaki sent Poncho a text that read, "Tonight." A minute later Poncho replied, "That's what I'm talking about, amigo." It was about to be some serious work call.

S. Allen

Chapter 13

"99 on the lane, fam!" Poobee yelled to a Disciple gang member standing in front of the Robert Taylor Projects. Poobee was on security letting the Disciples knew that the police had just rolled by. The building he was securing was the 4950 building, a strong hold for the Disciple had the project pumping, making no less than $20,000 a day off the hustle.

Mr. Biggs let one of the Disciples who went by the name of Max G run the operation, giving him lieutenant status. Max G's position was that of Governor as he had control over the projects. It was Max G who turned in $250,000 a month to Mr. Biggs. Mr. Biggs liked how he conducted business and how the Disciples operated. It was one way into the projects. Security was tight on the back of the building, on full alert for police as well as rival gang members that the Disciples were at war with.

Pedro had been on security for an hour and a half when Lil Blue walked up to relieve him of his shift. It was 9:30 at night and Poobee was trying to bounce. He had a chick he was trying to go see and with the night still young, if he hurried, he could be up in some pussy soon.

"What's good, fam?"

"Me, sometimes you." Poobee and Lil' Blue shook hands the Disciple way before Poobee handed him the 45-ACP that was concealed on his waist.

"Alright bro, I'm gone, be safe." Poobee made his way to his Chevy Caprice.

"Aye fam!"

Poobee turned around.

"You already know I'ma be out here for a few hours. You got some of that Molly on you?"

Poobee looked at Lil' Blue sideways. "You tripping. You know niggas ain't supposed to be under the influence while on security!. That's law!" He said reminding Lil' Blue of the laws and policies the Disciple were governed by.

"Come on, my nigga. I be super on point when I'm on that shit." Blue retorted. Poobee was reluctant he give Lil' Blue the Molly which was the pure form of Ecstasy.

Lil' Blue went in his pocket and pulled out a wad of cash and peeled of two twenties and handed them to Poobee.

"Be careful out here, fam." Poobee warned, looking Lil' Blue in his eyes, letting him know he was serious.

"Don't even trip, G, I get this."

Poobee jumped into his whip and pulled off leaving Lil' Blue to hold down the post.

Lil' Blue swallowed the two pills and chased it down with the half bottle of Hennessy he had. Scanning the parking lot he saw a white Benz. At that moment he knew the big homie Max G was in the building. It was going to be a long night. Lil' Blue sat on an empty milk carton and watched the activity in front of the building, making sure everything was running smoothly.

The streets at the southside was in full motion on the Low-end. This area of the city was called the Low-end because of the low street numbers. The crime rate in the city was high due to the drug and gang activity. With so many different gangs in the neighborhood, beef was inevitable as the gangsters clashed over drug sales and territory, using automatic weapons to defend their empires. The Mayor of the City of Chicago at the time was Mayor Swolley and had tagged this area of the city as a red zone for violent crime.

The projects on the Low-end ran from 22nd Street 51st Street. The gangs had turned the low-income projects into forts for their drug distribution. Mayor Swolley felt the only way to bring down the extensive murder rate was to do away with the Chicago Housing Authority and destroy the projects and build condos in its place, forcing the blacks who were on Section 8 funding to relocate to different areas of the city, and replacing them with middle class citizens. The procedure would take years to complete. But until then the bloodshed and drugs would continue to be a problem.

It was late at night, and the weather was beginning to break into the spring season. The smells of exhaust and restaurants polluted the air. Cars banging loud sound systems could be heard as well as small unsupervised children playing in the streets. Homeless people stood on corners begging for change, only to get enough coins to purchase some cheap wine to get their shakes off. The Low-end was the epic of the poverty-stricken city.

Lil' Blue stood on his post doing security. Molly and the liquor had him feeling good as the drug went through his blood stream. His attention was diverted when a thick hood rat from the projects named Kiesha walked up on him. She was a sack chaser and was always trying to get Lil' Blue to get her high. He had been trying to get in her panties since 8th grade and the way he was feeling off the Molly he started to think with his small head instead of his big head.

"Aye, Kiesha, do me a favor and run to the store and get me some blunts and a grape soda." He pulled off a $10 bill from his bankroll and handed it to her, who looked like she had just hit the lottery. She couldn't wait to get back so she could get high for free. Lil' Blue watched her as she made her way to the Amoco gas station. He was definitely trying to slide up in Keisha's wet walls.

"Excuse me, youngsta. We trying to get some dope."

Lil' Blue was startled when he turned around. He hid the two bands suspiciously all while gripping the handle of the Sig. Covering his nose from the stench of the two fiends, he said, "On the first floor," and nodded toward the building.

"Thanks, youngsta." One of the fiends replied scratching his nappy long dreads before they walked off toward the 4950 buildings.

Lil' Blue focused his attention back on the girl he sent to the store. Molly had him feeling good. And totally off his square.

The two fiends made their way inside of the building. The smell of urine and weed smoke hung in the air inside the trashy hallway. About 6 Disciples were on the first floor involved in an intense dice game. A large pool of cash was in the middle of the circle. One of the thugs looked up at the fiends as he shook the red dice in his hand, seeing that they were nothing more than drunks he turned back to the game, rolling the dice as the two men made their way to the sixth floor of the projects.

"The sixth floor, amigo. Apartment 60," Poncho said, pulling the small silenced assault rifle from the dirty trench coat he wore.

Malaki followed suit, screwing the silencer on his Glock. The dirty dreads he had hung over his face as he ascended the stairs.

A song from Meek Mill banged from the Bose sound system. Max G had a blunt of Sour Diesel Kush hanging from his lips as he tied a thick red rubber band around a stack of small bills. He was accompanied by 2 more Disciples— Wax and JD— who were breaking down and bagging up pounds of weed. Max G tossed the rubber banded stack into a duffle bag with the rest of the drug money. He had been the Governor for the Disciples since his older brother Jilla was killed in a drug deal gone bad. At that moment he chose to follow in his brothers' footsteps and dive head-first into the violent drug game. Those who were subordinate to him looked to him as a teacher. It was because of him they were able to compete in the game. With the best weed in the Midwest, the Disciples brought in plenty of money. Max G was a smart hustler. When Mr. Biggs and his men tried to bring war to the Disciples over the 4950 building which was a gold mine, Max G used his diplomatic politics. They could've gone to war with the Body Snatchers, but that would have slowed up the money. The purpose of the Disciples as a whole was to make money. Max G had his mind set on the future. He would use Mr. Biggs as a stepping stone to get his weight up and then he would venture into his own endeavors. And if Mr. Biggs and his goon felt some kind of way, the Disciples would be ready, locked and loaded.

Malaki and Poncho stood outside apartment 602. They knew they were at the right apartment. Poncho had given a young cat $1,000 for the information. They knew Max G was in the apartment. Everything was going as planned. Poncho pulled the slide back on the Draco AK-47 while Malaki pounded on the door.

"Somebody at the door?" Max G asked turning the stereo down. The door was pounded twice again. He got up from the couch to answer the door; a 38 Special was clutched in his right hand. "These lil' niggas be tweaking." Max stated thinking it was one of the Disciples coming to get more weed. Without looking out the peephole he opened the door.

Malaki brought the handle of the Glock over Max's mouth. It split instantly; Max's gun fell to the floor. They stepped inside the small apartment with their weapons extended in front of them, ready to discharge. JD reached for the Springfield Armory XD that was in his reach. The slug from Malaki's gun penetrated his right hand. Poncho closed the door behind them. Max was still holding his broken nose that was bleeding profusely. Max G sat frozen on the couch like a popsicle. Dondo pointed the body choppa at him; his trigger finger itching.

"Do you work for Mr. Biggs?" Malaki questioned.

"Naw, man. Why? What's up?" Max G replied, shaking like dice in a craps game.

Malaki raised his Glock and pulled the trigger, hitting Max G in the kneecap. Max G let out a piercing scream as he saw the gaping hole in his knee. "Now I ask you again. Do. You. Work for Mr. Biggs?" Max G nodded his head yes. "Where can I find him?"

"I don't know, man. I promise you. I'm nothing but a worker. I just collect his breed. I swear." Max G pleaded, hoping he could get out of the situation with his life.

Poncho trained his weapon in Max and JD.

Malaki looked around the living room, noticing the pounds of weed and over 1,000 small dime bags of the exotic marijuana. "You made one mistake."

"What's that?" Max G painfully asked through clenched teeth. Pain shooting through his body.

"Dealing with Mr. Biggs," Malaki said and applied pressure to the trigger.

***

Lil' Blue had just lit the freshly rolled blunt of Kush and handed it to Keisha. She took a pull of the potent weed letting the THC invade her lungs. She started to have a coughing fit as the smoke in her chest squeezed her lungs like vice grips. Lil' Blue looked toward the front of the building. It had been over 10 minutes since the fiends went in. The Molly had tweaked his mood as it went from lust to now paranoia. Something wasn't right, his Spidey senses had just knocked in, scanning the street for any law enforcement.

Seeing none he grabbed the blunt back from Keisha. "I'll be right back, shorty." Lil' Blue made his way to the project building, leaving Keisha standing there fuming. Walking in the building he saw his homies shooting dice. "Where them fiends that came in here a minute go?" He questioned taking a pull from his blunt.

"They went upstairs." Baby Dro said as he rolled the dice.

"Man. Why the fuck they go upstairs? Ain't no dope on no other floor!" Lil' Blue grabbed the gun off his waist. He knew something wasn't right. By them not being on point the security had been breached. "Y'all can do that shit later." He said referring to the dice game. "Come with me to the 6th floor," he commanded his men. The gangsters obliged and followed Lil' Blue up the stair well.

Malaki slung the duffle bag over his right shoulder.

"What you doing, amigo?"

"We taking all money. Right?" Malaki asked.

"No, Eśe, we come out of the building with the bag they will sense some foul play, and we might not make it out. Understand?"

Malaki dropped the bag to the floor. Max G was slumped on the couch with a bullet embedded in his head. JD was also executed in the same order. The smell of death was thick in the small apartment.

"Let's go, my friend." Poncho turned the doorknob, opening the door only to come face to face with Lil' Blue and a few of his people about the knock on the door.

Sensing bullshit Lil' Blue raised his gun. Malaki and Poncho was caught off guard. Looking over Poncho's shoulder Lil' Blue saw the stiff corpse of his boss with his brains leaking. Lil' Blue slapped Poncho's face. Malaki and Poncho did as they were in-structed. The Discipline searched them and relieve them of their weapons.

"Who the fuck y'all niggas with?" Lil' Blue interrogated. A grave mistake when dealing with Malaki and Poncho, they came talking instead of killing. This mistake would cost Lil' Blue his life.

Poncho brought his knee up to Lil' Blues nut sack. Lil' Blue yelled like a stray dog; his pain was excruciating. One of the Disciples fired his weapon at Poncho as Poncho pulled Lil' Blue close to him, using him as a human shield. He took 8 slugs to the chest. The Discipline pulled a gun but was too late. Malaki grabbed his arm and sent a strong roundhouse to the thug's mid-section, knocking the wind out of him from a broken rib cage. Picking up the thug's weapon, Malaki fired a hot slug into his face, pushing his wig back. Picking up his silenced rifle, Poncho sprayed led at the fleeing gang members trying to escape from the two killers. Three of them caught slugs in the back.

"Shit!" Poncho yelled in frustration. A few of the goons had gotten away.

Malaki grabbed his Glock off the ground.

"Let's go, Malaki." Poncho made his way down the steps.

Malaki followed him, walking past one of a dying Disciple who was still holding onto his life. Malaki fired a round into the man's head, silencing him forever without breaking his stride, disappearing into the city's darkness like ghosts.

S. Allen

Chapter 14

"You mean to tell me some crack heads killed Max G and his men?" Mr. Biggs' voice thundered in the confines of his office as he slammed his fist on the oakwood desk. The two Disciples who got away from the hands of the reapers stood before him, telling what they witnessed. Killa Fred and Body Bag remained stood before him, telling him what they witnessed.

Killa Fred and Body Bag remained silent, listening to every word. Mr. Biggs picked up a copy of the Chicago Tribune for the third time. The killings had made the headline. *"Massacre in Robert Taylors claims two lives."* The media was giving the murders extra attention.

"Police say they found money and drugs. So this wasn't no robbery shit. So it has to be personal." Mr. Biggs started tossing the paper on the desk. "Where was the security? How did they managed to get to the 6th floor without being detected?"

The two gangsters remained silent. They knew they had fucked up in a major way. They weren't on point. Instead they were shooting dice. Lovelle and Marko was scared shitless as Mr. Biggs stared at them through bloodshot eyes. Resembling the devil. Marko had told Lovelle on the way to Mr. Biggs' office about the lil' dude from the building named Charlie Boy. He was seen getting out of a silver Range Rover a few weeks prior to the incident at the Robert Taylors. Charlie Boy was only 14 years old. The Disciples used him to run errands as well as watch for the police while they sold their drugs. With his mother being strung out on heroin, Charlie Boy had to fend for himself, looking up to the gangsters in his hood.

Marko found it odd when he saw Charlie Boy hop out the expensive SUV. It didn't dawn on him until they were on the way to the office that Charlie Boy could possible know something about the murders.

Mr. Biggs walked form behind his desk. A chrome 44 revolver in his hands. Opening the cylinder to the thunder cannon he turned it upside down. The shells fell into the palm of his left hand. Putting one of the hollow points back into the cylinder he spent it and locked it. With only one bullet in the gun he turned it to Lavelle. "Nobody got shit to say, huh?" He put the chrome to Lavelle's hot neck.

"Fam, I don't know. We never saw them niggas before." Lavelle stuttered.

Mr. Biggs pulled trigger. *Click!* Marko let out a breath of relief that his brain still rested in his cranium. Now standing behind Lavelle he passed the 44 to the back of his skull. Lavelle's legs were about to give out. Body Bag snickered looking at the performance in front of him.

"Are you going to answer the question? Or is it something you not telling me, boy?" Mr. Biggs said through clenched teeth. His anger growing by the moment, just at the sight of the fake gangsters.

"We were shooting dice, and didn't notice them come in the building!" Lavelle blurted out. Mr. Biggs pulled the trigger. "Ahhhh!" Lavelle yelled as he came face to face with death.

Mr. Biggs was now pointing the hammer to Marko's dome. "Were you at the dice game too?"

Marko knew if the wrong thing came out his mouth, he would be a dead issue. He would use this time to get his life spared. "Mr. Biggs. It's this lil' dude in our projects. His name Charlie Boy. I saw him a few weeks ago getting out of a suspicious Range Rover that was parked in front of our building. The windows were tinted so I couldn't see in the truck. But something wasn't right." Marko stuttered.

"What is the boy's name again?"

"His name is Charlie Boy."

Mr. Biggs nodded at Body Bag and Killa Fred. More work didn't have to be explained. Turning his attention back to Marko he pulled the trigger. *BOOOOOM!* The powerful handguns recoiled, causing it to jerk in Mr. Biggs' hand. The hollow point round blew Marko's brains through the back of his hand in a pinkish mist, releasing brain tissue and skull fragments before his body dropped to the floor. Mr. Biggs spat on the corpse. Sitting back at his desk he laid the smoking murder wean down. The smell of fresh spilled blood was in the air. "Now. You two. Find this boy and find out who was in that Range Rover. This shit cannot continue. I'm loosing money. And when I lose money, niggas lose their lives."

"What you want us to do with this nigga?" Body Bag asked nodding toward Lavelle who had pissed his Louis Vuitton jeans. His man's brains splattered on the side of his face. Mr. Biggs looked at Body Bag like he was high on stupidity. Body Bag got the hint. "Yeah, you right big homie. What kind of question is that?" Grabbing Lovelle by his Polo shirt Body Bag spat a razor from his mouth, running it across the center of Lovelle's neck. The sharp razor cut like butter. Lavelle gargled on his own blood. Fell to his knees grabbing at his throat. DNA sprayed all over Body Bag's Gucci sneakers. "Damn, I paid 2 stacks for these." He said jumping back. Levelle died only seconds later.

"Clean up this mess. And find that boy." Mr. Biggs ordered to his murderous henchmen.

***

Charlie Boy had just come from Aldi's grocery store doing some shopping. He filled the refrigerator as well as the kitchen cupboards. It had been a minute since he had some food in his home, due to his mother's drug habit. She would get government checks every 1st of the month, but would spend it all getting high, thus leaving starving pain in Charlie Boy's stomach. It seems the only way he could get some food was by hanging around the dope boys in his building. He wasn't a tough guy so joining the gang wasn't even up for discussion. Charlie Boy was in the 9th grade of Dumber High School. He excelled in his academics but hated going to school because of his poor wardrobe that consisted of two pairs of pants, the three shirts and a pair of beat up Scottie Pippen's. All that changed a few days ago when a silver Range Rover pulled up on him when he was walking home from the gas station. The passenger of the truck flashed a thick wad of cash. Charlie's stomach was in his back and with just a couple dollars of the money he could feed his hunger. The Mexican man told him to get in the backseat. Looking around, thinking about his next meal he climbed into the backseat of the Range Rover. The driver, a brown skinned man, pulled the whip into the congested traffic.

"What y'all want with me?" Charlie Boy asked admiring the interior of the SUV.

The Mexican handed him half of the wad of cash.

Charlie Boy thumbed through the 10s, 20s and 50s.

"Do you know who Max G is that stays in your building?" The Mexican asked.

"Yeah, I know him." He stuffed the bills in his dirty Levi's.

"What apartment does he stay in?" Malaki asked from behind the wheel, eyeing Charlie Boy in the rear-view mirror.

"Apartment 602. The weed floor." He responded.

Malaki nodded. Poncho gave Charlie Boy the rest of the stack of cash. Malaki pulled back in front of the 4950 building.

"That's all y'all want?" Charlie Boy reached for the door handle.

"Thank you for your cooperation, Eśe," said Poncho.

"Alright." Charlie Boy hopped out the truck.

That was days ago. Heading out the door in his new Nike sweat suit, new Jordan's laced his feet, he was feeling good and wanted to go outside to stunt his newfound wealth. Walking to the dollar store on 43rd and State where he knew he would run into some girls from his school he heard music banging from a vehicle. The thunderous speakers seem to shake the concrete as the black Tahoe came to a screeching halt on the side of him. The back door was swung open. Charlie watched in confusion as a tall man with dreads hopped out and grabbed him into the truck. Charlie Boy's scream never left his lungs. The door closed and the truck sped off.

Chapter 15

Malaki slid the Buick Lacrosse through the city's traffic. He was in a down mood as he made his way to the Burr-Oaks Cemetery. Commander Sanchez told him where his parents were buried. Even though he would never meet them in the physical he was going to be in touch with them in the spiritual. With a lot on his mind Malaki had some important business to handle with Poncho and wouldn't let his emotions take a toll on him. He and Poncho were leaving a trail of destruction as well as bodies. Malaki was starting to question the strategy they were using and if they were even close to Mr. Biggs.

Pulling into the parking lot of the cemetery Malaki killed the engine, rested his head on the headrest, and closed his eyes. The violence was starting to tear his nerves, but nevertheless his ambition to kill Mr. Biggs outweighed his conscious. Grabbing the bouquet of flowers from the backseat he exited the vehicle. The sun was shining and the weather was warm. It was a perfect day. Looking at the piece of paper in his hand Malaki located his parents' gravesites that were next to each other. Malaki read his parents' headstones and stared at the picture of his deceased father that sat on the tombstone. The small picture was like he was looking in a mirror. Seeing his own reflection. The American flag laid folded in its vigil. The picture was a small picture that Bryan took when he was in the Army. He saw the picture numerous times. It was that picture that made him so proud of his father, not to mention the countless war stories that Commander Sanchez had told him about his father.

Malaki laid some flowers of his father's vigil. Taking a knee at his mother's tombstone he graced his eyes on her beautiful picture. She was so beautiful. He didn't know much about his mother, nothing more than his father was madly in love with her, and that she died by the bullets that was meant for him. She was a casualty of war between Bryon and Mr. Biggs, but Malaki lived through it, and that mistake would cost all that was involved. Malaki wiped the warm tear that fell from his eye with the back of his hand as he laid the remaining flowers on his mother's tombstone and kissed it.

Standing up he looked up to the beautiful blue sky. The sun warmed his face as he closed his eyes. "Momma. Father. I want you to know that I love you with all of my breath that I breathe. I know you are looking down on me from the heavens above. You may be mad at me. Or you may be proud of me. You are my ambition for what I do. I will not rest until justice is served to the evil men who have caused this— caused your lives to be lost and me to suffer from not having you in my life. Momma. Father. I love you. Look over me in all of my trials and tribulations. I love you."

Wiping his last tear Malaki silently prayed for his parents and vowed he would shed no more tears. Opening his eyes that were now the color of fresh blood, it was time to step it up a notch. Mr. Biggs would be the grand finale in the game of murder and revenge. His life was on borrowed time and the clock was ticking, but the retired Detective Michael Calhoun's time was up, too. The reaper had called his number and it was time for him to serve his death sentence. Pulling out of the lot of the cemetery Malaki got his cell phone and dialed Poncho's number.

"Como estas, amigo!"

"Poncho, I need a favor."

"Anything, my friend." Poncho replied.

"I need to meet up with you at your apartment later tonight. I'm thinking about 11:30?" Malaki said putting on his turn signal and switching lanes.

"Why not come over now?"

"I can't now, Poncho, I have somebody I have to meet. But I will call you when I'm done."

"No problem, my friend. I'll be here waiting on you."

It was 12:15 and Malaki was running late. He had made plans with Nicki to meet her at the Navy Pier. He couldn't wait to see her face. Her beauty alone made him smash the gas.

Poncho got off the phone with Malaki and finished his last set of Navy Seal push-ups. After wiping the sweat from his face with a towel, and getting a bottled water from the fridge, he downed half the bottle to quench his thirst. Poncho was wondering what kind of favor Malaki needed. Hearing the anxiousness on Malaki's voices had his interest piqued. He guessed he would find out soon enough.

Poncho knew they had to bring the war with the Body Snatchers to an end and put Mr. Biggs in a body bag. The murders of the Robert Taylor's brought extreme heat to the city streets. It was rumored that the Feds stepped in and started investigating the homicides. Poncho smiled at the thought of the killing and how it was carried it out. The disguises they used was impeccable.

Poncho and Malaki pulled up on two drunks who were begging for change on the northside of the city. Poncho got out and approached the two bums.

"Youngin, can you spare a quarter?" The bum shook his change cup that was nothing but a Coca-Cola can cut in half.

Poncho pulled out two long bundles of cash that was wrapped in rubber bands. The two bums' eyes got big like they had just taken a hit of coke. Poncho smiled. "Let me get your clothes, amigo."

The two homeless men looked at each other in confusion, and with the speed of light started to undress. Right on the sidewalk. After stripping, the men threw their clothes in a pile in front of Poncho. As they stood in dirty underwear, Poncho tossed them the two stacks of cash.

"God bless your soul, youngsta." One of the bums said revealing a mouth full of rotten teeth. The two of them took off running with the cash like they were at a track meet. Straight to the nearest dope boy or liquor store. Or Bath.

Scooping up the pile of clothes that reeked of must and funk he got back in the car, tossing the clothes in the backseat.

Malaki covered his nose, not wanting to breathe the foul smell. "What's all that about?" Malaki asked.

Poncho laughed. "That, my friend, is our way into the projects." He pulled into traffic.

Poncho smiled at the thought of his brilliance. Walking in his room he grabbed the black book. The book of death. They had some more names to cross off. And time was ticking.

Pulling into the parking lot, Malaki parked next to a dark blue BMW. The Navy Pier parking lot wasn't crowded and Nicki's car wasn't hard to spot. Looking over at her he smiled. She returned a Colgate smile of her own. Malaki got out the car. Her Mariah Carey perfume greeted him before she even got close. Now standing in front of him, Nicki's beauty was intoxicating. Stepping back, he took in the goddess that stood before him. Nicki was dressed conservatively yet sexy. Her jeans were tight. It looked as if they were painted on her flesh. The six-inch Prada pumps made her seem taller than the last time he saw her. Her silky black hair was tied into a neat ponytail bringing out her gorgeous facial features. Strawberry MAC lip gloss coated her full lips. She was definitely a dime piece.

"Why you staring at me like that, boy?" Nicki asked shyly.

Malaki shook her beauty off, coming back to reality. "Oh. I'm sorry. I mean no disrespect. It's just. You are so beautiful." Malaki responded truthfully.

Nicki batted her long eyelashes. "That's so sweet of you to say. You definitely got it going on yourself boo." Nicki said seductively looking Malaki up and down.

Malaki was rocking a dark pair of Tru Religion jeans. The black Air Max boots gave him a thuggish yet Boss appeal. The black Ferragamo button up fitted his muscular frame just right. Nicki was pleased at the sight of him.

The two sat at a restaurant called Goose Island that served the best seafood the city had to offer. Malaki ordered the shrimp Carrabelle as Nicki opted for the fried catfish and baked macaroni. They were waiting for their food.

Nicki took a sip of her water. "So, Mr. Malaki. Is there a reason you were 30 minutes late?"

Malaki looked up. Caught off guard by her question. "My apologies. I was at the cemetery."

"Cemetery? If you don't mind me asking, why were you at the cemetery?"

The waiter set their hot meals on the table. "Is there anything I can get you guys?"

"No, thank you." Nicki said.

"If you need anything just let me know." The waitress walked off leaving them with their privacy.

Nicki stared at Malaki, waiting for him to answer her question. "No, I don't mind. I went to visit my deceased parents." he dug into his food.

"Oh, I'm sorry, Malaki. Were you close with them?"

"I never got a chance to meet them. My mother was shot while she was pregnant with me. The doctors couldn't save her, but they managed to save me. My father was killed a few days later." Malaki said putting a fork full of Carrabolla in his mouth.

"Oh my God, Malaki, I had no idea. I'm sorry for questioning you like that; you have been through so much, baby." Nicki said shocked by what Malaki had just told her. She wanted nothing more at that moment than to be there for him.

"It's okay, Nicki. Your food is getting cold, beautiful." Malaki said switching the subject.

"It looks great." Nicki tasted her macaroni and cheese. "I think you're a nice person, Malaki. You seem to be a strong black man. Why don't you have a wife?"

"How you know I don't?" Malaki joked.

"Boy, don't make me hurt you!" Nicki said playfully, hitting Malaki on the shoulder.

"Nah, I'm joking. I guess I never had a chance to get to know a woman like that."

"I feel you; life is just so busy." Nicki replied staring Malaki in his brown eyes.

"You know, sometimes you have to let love just fall and land in your lap," Malaki shot back, looking Nicki in her eyes.

Nicki was caught up, she was falling for Malaki hard. "I guess so," Nicki retorted.

After finishing their meals, they decided to walk to Buckingham Fountains. Malaki had his arm draped around Nicki's shoulder while Nicki held on to his waist.

"So, what do you do besides beat people up in restaurants?" Nicki asked looking up at him.

"Protect women named Nicki." Malaki stated quick on his feet.

Nicki leaned in and kissed him on his lips. Malaki tasted her strawberry lip gloss as the tongue was warm and succulent. He hugged her tightly. At that moment nothing else in the world mattered. She had his undivided attention and he didn't seem to mind.

Nicki broke the long, passionate kiss. "You something else, Malaki."

Malaki responded by kissing her. They kicked it in downtown Chicago for another hour before they walked back to their vehicles. Nicki wanted Malaki to follow her back to her condo. Malaki respectfully declined her request. He had to meet up with Poncho for something important, and he was letting nothing get in the way of that. Malaki kissed her lips promising he would see her very soon. She nodded in understanding. Her love box was on fire and only Malaki could put it out. She wanted him. She just hoped and prayed that he wanted her the same.

Chapter 16

"Wake your ass up, shorty. Nap time is over!" Body Bag stated after slapping Charlie Boy across the face, who was bound and tied in the chair in a basement in a abandoned building on the Westside.

Both of his eyes were swollen shut from the hellacious beating he took from the Body Snatcher. The punishment they inflicted was vicious. Charlie Boy took a breath as the pain shot through his lungs from his broken ribs. Body Bag and Killa Fred stood before them with two of the Body Snatchers gang members.

Body Bag had gotten the call from Quiet Storm letting them know they had snatched Charlie Boy up. That was the info that they needed. The sooner they found out the identity and whereabouts of the man responsible for the murder of Max G, the sooner they could crush them and continue with the business of getting back to the money. Body Bag lit a Newport and took a strong pull from the cancer stick. He was in murder mode dressed in army fatigue from head to toe. Butter wheat Timb's adorned his feet, while two . 45 caliber Glocks were in holsters on his shoulders.

Killa Fred walked over to Charlie Boy, who was trying to speak, but the duct tape on his mouth made his attempt futile. Killa Fred grabbed Charlie Boy's bruised and battered face. It was remotely dark in the basement but Killa Fred was visible as the diamonds in his chain and on his wrist brought a sense of light into the darkness. Killa Fred snatched the tape from Charlie Boy's mouth.

"Please, I want to go home to my momma." Charlie Boy cried with tears rolling from his eyes.

"In due time, my son but first, I'm going to ask you some simple questions. I'm going to need some simple answers. Do you understand?"

Charlie Boy nodded weakly.

"Very good. Now, who was it that you were in the Range Rover with a few days ago?"

"I don't know." Charlie Boy responded.

"Wrong answer!" Killa Fred slapped Charlie Boy with his diamond pinky ring cutting a deep gash in Charlie Beys face.

"Now, I'm going to ask you again. If you want to make it back home to your mother, I suggest you tell us the truth. Your lying will only cause complications for yourself. Who was the motherfuckers in the truck and how do you know them?" Killa Fred asked through clenched teeth. Charlie Boy tried to calm himself before he spoke.

"I don't know them. They just pulled up on me and."

"And what?"

"They shoved me a lot of money. They asked me did I know 'Max G' and what apartment he was in. I told them he be in 602 and then they gave me one thousand dollars. I was hungry, man." Charlie Boy confessed.

"They didn't say who they were?"

"No sir. Can I please go home? I'm scared."

"How did they look?" Killa Fred asked.

"One was black and the other one was Mexican. I never saw them around before." Charlie Boy said truthfully.

"See, that wasn't so bad was it?" Killa Fred patted him on the head like a puppy who had just fetched the morning paper. He pulled Body Bag to the side.

"The lil' nigga telling the truth but what he saying ain't much, you dig?" Killa Fred stated, looking back at Charlie Boy.

Body Bag flicked his cigarette to the ground before smashing it with his Timberland boot.

"You think whoever it was in the truck is the same niggas that put down the other demonstrations?" Body Boy blew out a thick cloud of smoke.

"It ain't no secret. The thing is we gotta find out at who they are and punish them niggas before this shit get outta hand. You already know the streets is watching. I'm make a few phone calls because we gotta fix this shit. And fast. Let's get up outta here." Killa Fred made his way up the stairs. Body Bag looked up to his two soldiers and nodded toward Charlie Boy.

A gunshot rang out. A smile came across Body Bag's face. Whoever was bringing them difficulties better had liked the movies. They were about to get front row seats to the Murda Show.

Poncho poured a glass of Jose Cuervo Tequila and took a seat on the couch across from Malaki, who was texting on his phone to Nicki. He couldn't wait to see her again.

"So, my friend, what is the most important favor you need from me?" Poncho asked, getting right to the point.

"I need a block at C-4." Malaki replied not even looking up from his phone. Poncho looked at Malaki with a raised eyebrow.

"What you need C-4 for, Eśe?"

"I guess somebody made me mad." Malaki stated. Poncho downed the rest of his liquor. The strong liquid warmed his insides.

"My friend, when do we start keeping secrets from each other? We have been truthful in our events. No?" Malaki sent his text and put his phone in his jacket.

"Poncho, Mr. Biggs is both of our targets, but the situation of mine is personal. It has nothing to do with you. No disrespect." Malaki said. His demeanor was serious as Cancer. Poncho stared at Malaki. He knew a warrior when he saw one. Malaki was a trained killer with morals and ambition. He also knew being a warrior that Malaki would never break his morals or principles. He liked Malaki and considered him a true friend as well as a comrade in arms. He wanted to know more about this solo mission that Malaki was trying to carry out, but figured he wouldn't pressure the young killer. If Malaki wanted to put him on the hit, he would let him know. Until then, he would let Malaki do him.

"You killing me with all the quiet shit, amigo." Poncho started before disappearing into the bathroom.

"Nothing personal, Poncho. Just business.

"Como quieros!"

"What does that mean?"

"Whatever." Poncho yelled from the backroom. Malaki just shook his head. He knew his friend was in his feelings but he knew he would get over it. In the game of murder feelings needed to be nonexistent. Poncho returned with an Orange Nike Box and handed it to Malaki. Taking the lid off, Malaki examined the clay piece of C-4 that sat in the box between two pieces of Styrofoam.

"You are going to have to make your own detonator. You do know what you are doing with that, don't you?" Malaki paid Poncho no mind as he continued to study the explosive device. Commander Sanchez had trained him in explosives and he knew that C-4 was a beast. A chill ran down his spine as he thought of the evil and terror he was going to unleash on his enemies. The device he now held was going to crash his target completely.

"I'm just saying, Eśey. That shit ain't no joke." Malaki placed the top back in the box.

"Poncho, thank you. I will be forever in debt to you." Malaki started making his way to the front door.

"Yeah, yeah, just know we have some business to handle. More names on the death list. Bring us closer to Mr. Biggs," Poncho said. Malaki nodded his head with understanding and walked out of the house. He had a recipe to bake a cake, and once it was baked, he was going to blow out the candles. Literally.

***

"Hurry hurry up, we're running late," Valie said, putting on her gold hoop earrings. Today was the day their beautiful daughters Mane and Valie would walk across the stage and graduate from the University of Illinois.

"I'm comin', hun," Michael Calhoun replied as he sprayed on some Cool Water cologne. Starring in the mirror at his reflection, he noticed the spider webs on the sides of his eyes. His hair was slicked back but yet the strands of grey were visible to anyone who had 2020 vision. The years on the Chicago streets as a Homicide Detective had taken a toll on him. Even though he had been retired for almost twenty years, his physical appearance was a constant reminder of his time served. At 60, he felt that mentally he was in his prime. He was a devoted husband as well as a proud father of two beautiful girls." The thought of them pursuing their dreams made him smile.

"The reception isn't for another hour. We have plenty time, sweetie."

"Yeah, I know, but I want to get their early so we can get some good seats." Valie slapped her Coach purse over her shoulder. Putting on his navy blue blazer, Michael Calhoun took one last look at his appearance to make sure everything was intact and on point. He went downstairs to meet his wife in the living room. Valie waited impatiently for her slow husband. Michael walked up and kissed her on her lips, embracing her.

"I'm so proud of the girls, Val. They did it, babe."

"Yes they did, Michael. Now they can become successful, huh?" Maybe take care of us old folks." Valie said with a smile.

"That's the plan." Michael retorted.

"Hold on, sweetie. I forgot my phone." Valie went back upstairs to retrieve her iPhone, as Michael went to start the car.

Walking outside, the warm Chicago weather greeted Michael Calhoun. His neighbor's poodle began to bark hysterically at Michael while he was tied to his chain in the yard. Michael smiled and picked up the Chicago Tribune that the paperboy had thrown on the porch a few hours ago. Michael hit the alarm to unlock the doors to his Mercedes Sedan. The car was a gift to himself when he retired from the force, it was his pride and joy. After sticking the key in the ignition, the engine came to life. Valie was locking the front door to the house. Michael Calhoun sense something was wrong. He was smelling smoke and noticed it coming from under the hood of the Mercedes. He was about to get out and inspect it until *BOOOOOOM!*

Valie was blown to the door from the impact of the explosion. Debris and metal covered the street. Gaining her conscious back, Valie looked at the grave site before her.

"Michael!" She yelled at the site of the burning Mercedes. She knew that her husband was dead. Falling to her knees, she let out a piercing scream for help as the tears ran down her face.

Malaki drove past the Calhoun residence in the tinted Range Rover. He had detonated the C-4 that he placed under the ex-detective's Benz the night before. Michael Calhoun had taken his father's life and he now had paid the ultimate price, with his own life. Looking through the tint, Malaki saw Calhoun's grieving wife. They had something in common. The grief from losing a loved one.

Chapter 17

"I'm John Alveraz."

"And I'm Vanessa Johnson, and you're tuned into WGN News at 10. On today's top story federal authorities are investigating the assassination of retired Homicide Detective Michael Calhoun. Authorities say the 20-year veteran started his car this morning and the vehicle exploded. Let's go to Dionte Collins, who is live at the scene where the officer received this deadly fate. Dionte, can you tell watchers what's going on in the murder of Michael Calhoun?"

"Thank you, Vanessa. I'm at the site where the explosion happened. Right here, we are looking at the exploded vehicle. It appears that the retired Detective was sitting in his car waiting for his wife so they could attend their daughter's graduation ceremony when the car burst into a ball of flames, claiming his life. After investigating, bomb squad workers were able to find what looks to be pieces of an explosion device. Authorities would like anybody with information on this horrific crime to please notify police."

"Thank you, Dionte."

"You're welcome."

"In other news today."

Malaki hit the button on the remote to turn the TV off. The breaking news invaded every station he turned to. Avenging his father's death seem to knock a load off of his book, but Mr. Biggs and the Body Snatchers weighed heavy on his mind. Mr. Biggs' burial was in the making and when the time presented itself, he would lay the dirt over the casket. Malaki's thoughts of homicide were interrupted when he heard a knock at the door.

"Knock Knock!" After grabbing his FNH Pistol off the dresser, he went to answer the door.

"Who is it?"

"Open up, Eśey. It's me Poncho." Malaki looked through the peephole only to see Poncho on the other side. Putting his weapon on his waist, Malaki opened the door.

"Damn, amigo! What took you so long to open the door?" Poncho said with a perplexed look on his face, holding a newspaper under his arms.

"You worried 'bout the wrong things, Eśe." Malaki stated sarcastically, stepping to the side to allow Poncho inside his living quarters.

"It seems your little secret has been exposed!" Poncho tossed the newspaper on the table.

Malaki picked it up. The headline story read: *Former Homicide Detective, Michael Calhoun Assassinated in Morning Car Bombing.*

Malaki's facial expression remained stone. "What does this have to do with secret missions?" he retorted, tossing the paper back on the table.

"No comprenda, huh? This killing has your name all over it."

"How do you figure that? My name is nowhere on the paper."

"You come to get C-4 from me. Then, the next day, some cop starts his car and BOOOMM. You not a good liar, my friend."

"He killed my father. He deserved his death." Malaki retired nonchalant as silence filled the air.

"My friend, I completely understand. Trust me. I know how it feels to have a father. I have lost mine. My father's death is my motivation to do what I do. Since we met, I have grown to care for you as a friend, and in the life that we live, real friends are almost extinct. So, when you find a real one, it is a must that you keep them close because you may never come across another one."

Malaki looked up at Poncho. "Malaki, always know that your fight is my fight. Your pain is my pain and your enemies are my enemies. We will crush them together as a team, compredna?" Malaki heard the genuine words that Poncho had spoken. He had genuine care for his safety and wellbeing. He had come to Chicago to kill. He hadn't anticipated on making any friendships. Being a trained killer didn't involve caring for others. Death was heartless and cold. Malaki seemed to have a soft spot in his heart for the Mexican assassin and also cared for his health.

"Don't worry, Poncho. Next time I decide to blow somebody up, I'll make sure to notify you first." Malaki joked.

"Whatever, Malaki, but anyway, I came over to holler at you about something else." Poncho pulled a map out of the pocket of his cargo pants. Unfolding it, he placed it on the table. "You see this plane here?" Poncho pointed to a section on the map that was circled in red maker. Malaki took a look close to what Poncho was talking about.

"What am I looking at?"

"My friend, this is a warehouse located in Green, Illinois. My boss has reason to believe this is a place where Mr. Biggs stores most of his drugs."

"So, what."

"What do you mean so what, essay? We destroy this place and Mr. Biggs loses out on a lot of money and it's a possibility he will be there." Malaki grabbed the bottom of his chin, pondering what he was saying.

"How do we get in, Poncho? Don't you think they gone be on point? Security and all?"

"My friend, they will never know what hit them. Trust me." Poncho replied with a sinister smirk on his face.

Body Bag walked around the conference table. His street lieutenants sat in attendance patiently waiting to see why the underboss had summoned them. These men were in charge of certain areas throughout the city where Mr. Biggs had his heroin distributed. Mr. Biggs and the Body Snatchers were involved in many endeavors in the drug game but the heroin was the source of riches that had he held down with an iron fist. Mr. Biggs had been adamant about stepping up the daily numbers on the heroin blocks because of the losses caused by the mysterious hitman. The Body Snatchers had to tighten up. Six of the drug dealers sat at the round table. Booveillie was in control of the lower end of the Southside. His particular block was 46th and Prairie all the way to 51st and Green. Also in attendance was J-Dirty, who controlled the Humboldt park area on the westside. J-Dirty was a loyal soldier to the Body Snatchers and had a major influence over the Hispanic community. Big D oversaw the Northside of the city. Then, you had Killa Cal, an old school cat just released from the FEDS, who maintained the eastside. His arm of the city was known as Terror-Town. Shorty Ruff and Face, who were identical twins, sat in silence. They where is charge of the suburb north of Chicago called Aurora.

Walking around the table with his hands clasped behind his back, BodyBag began to address the crew. He had a light Kevlar vest strapped over this crisp, white beater, his AKOO Jeans had a slight sag, while the gun on his waist was visible. Everybody at the table sat in anticipation.

"My nigga.I thank y'all for coming." The gang was in the basement of Wilson Furniture store that was owned by Mr. Biggs. Body Bag continued.

"Since our last sit down it has been a lot going on with our organization. As some of you might know, we have enemies that are bringing trouble and confusion upon us."

"Who we got beef with, fam?" One of the twins asked. Body Bag dreaded the question but knew it was unavoidable.

"That's a good question, Shorty Ruff. As of right now, all we know is we have been getting hit at some of our most lucrative spots. We have reason to believe that the two niggas are riding around in a Silver Range Rover. One Hispanic, one black. They managed to whack some of the Coke Boys on 78th Street." Body Bag looked at Boovellie. "Dive Dilla got knocked off coming from out of town and some of our GD'S associates were killed a few nights ago in their own projects. We think all the shit related.

"So, how we gon' kill a ghost?" Big D from the Northside intervened. The sarcasm in his voice irritated Body Bag.

"The point of this meeting is to put all of you on point. So that everybody is aware of what is going on and plus, it's going to be some amendments to the blocks. First and foremost, all blocks will close an hour early. No exceptions. Secondly, Mr. Biggs is putting an extra kilo on each block so y'all gon' have to grind extra hard to get it off. The losses we just took has to be made back. Period." Everybody nodded in understanding, all except for Big D.

"God damn, my nigga. Y'all want us to close shop early but y'all putting extra work on the block and we still gotta meet our quota? Make that make sense." Big D complained. Body Bag discreetly walked around the table and grabbed the baseball bat that was leaning against the wall. He never really like Big D. He felt he was a soft nigga, who had never put no work in for the organizations. But yet, always had something to say.

"Y'all should give us some extra time to get this money up."

"Yeah, my nigga. Take all the time you want," Body Bag replied before he raised the baseball bat and brung it down on Big D's skull. The aluminum bat to the back of Big D's head made a sickening sound that could be heard throughout the dimly lit basement. Body Bag repeatedly brought the bat down, crushing Big D's head in. Blood and pieces of brain splattered Killa Cob's face as he sat next to Big D. He wiped it off with the back of his hand. Body Bag was completely now out of breath. He stopped the assault and tossed the bloody bat on the floor. He wiped his soiled hands on his pants.

"Now, if it's anybody who feels the same way as this fat piece of shit, speak up!" Body Bag yelled. Nobody moved.

"Like I said, this shit getting real out here. Y'all motherfuckers better tighten up. Ain't no more losses getting took. A loss get took, a life get took. This meeting is adjourned." All the men stood and made an exit out of the building. All except Big D, who laid lifeless on the cold basement floor with his brains leaking out his melon. The example had been made. Body Bag grabbed his phone off the clip of his Gucci belt and dialed a number.

"Yeah, what's good, fam?" The man on the other line answered on the third ring.

"Cleanup on aisle three." Was Body Bag's only reply before he ended the call. He had a lot on his plate right now. It was his staff titles and duties that came with being Mr. Biggs' enforcer. His job was to enforce the law of the Body Snatchers. He had to pursue their enemies and appoint their proper punishment. He had a plan and if everything went accordingly, he would bring the so called hitman into the fold. And when he did, he would add them to the already extensive murder rate in the city. Body Bag lifted and jumped in his

whip. He had a lot to do and catching up with Lil' Tony was definitely on his to do list.

Chapter 18

Lil' Tony stood in between two abandoned buildings on the city's westside. A black Carhartt hoodie covered his head, while his hands inside the hoodie clutched a chrome 38 snub nose. It was late at night and Lil' Tony was trying to hustle off the last bundle of heroin that he had stashed in his sagging Rock Revival jeans. It had been months since his cousin Roni was murdered. Lil' Tony knew that what they were doing would catch up to them sooner or later. He had warned Ronnie about stealing from the Body Snatchers but his cousin failed to yield to his warning. In return, his life was claimed to the deadly streets of Chicago. Ronnie didn't even have the audacity to look out for him after the lick and now he was on the street alone and trying to survive at the same time. Going into hiding from the Body Snatchers, Lil' Tony moved to the Westside of the city. He was now a worker for a local drug dealer, who went by the name of Oso.

The blistering wind and below zero degree weather had Lil' Tony wanting to call it a night but the hustla in him wouldn't let him leave the block until the last of his drugs were sold. Lil' Tony eyed a skinny dope fiend making his way down the block in his direction.

"Blows! Blows! Blows!" Lil' Tony yelled, letting the fiend knew that he was posted in the cut and had that work. The fiend walked across the street toward Lil' Tony.

"What's good old head? I got them blows for your nose." The fiend walked up and pulled out some crumpled up bills.

"Let me get two for this thirteen, youngsta. Its' all I got, you dig." The dope fiend pleaded, hoping to get a deal for the two 10 dollar blows of heroin.

"Come up off the bread, old school. I knew you got some more money." Lil' Tony sneered, aggravated that the fiend came with short money.

"Come on now, youngster. You know I always shop over here. I'm just short. Let me get those two dimes to get this monkey off my back and I promise I'ma be back to spend some more money with ya." The dope fiend said, scratching his neck with his dirty hands. Pulling his stash out his jeans, Lil' Tony opened it and retrieved 2 pieces of folded aluminum foil.

"Man, don't make this shit no habit. You come on this block and I bet not see you copping from nobody else." Lil' Tony threatened while passing the fiend the drugs.

"Don't even trip, youngsta. Old school got you," The fiend replied before he dashed off to fill his veins with the potent drug. Lil' Tony added the crumbled up bills to the knot of cash that he had already accumulated that night and started walking toward the corner store to get a pack of cigarettes. He heard a familiar sound of a car speeding down the block. Looking up, he saw the black Crown Victoria pulling up and coming to a screeching halt. *Skuuurt.*

Detective Commander hopped out the Crown Vic pointing his 45 caliber Glock at Lil' Tony. Another unmarked car pulled up from out of nowhere.

"Let me see some hands!" The officer yelled pointing his weapon. Looking around, Lil' Tony saw he had nowhere to run. The block was now surrounded with Chicago's finest that would gun him down even if he had thought about running. Then, they would say he reached for the firearm that rested in his hoodie. It was surely a no win situation. Putting his hands up in the air, he took a knee in surrender. The officers rushed him and forcefully pushed him to the frozen concrete, scraping his face up in the process. After the cold handcuffs were slapped tightly on his wrist, he was relieved of his gun, the bundle of drugs as well as his cash.

"My, my, my," The officer said as if he was Johnny Gill, the singer from back in the early 90's.

"Looks like you got caught with the mother load." The officer then read Lil' Tony his Miranda Rights. Lil' Tony sat in the backseat with his head laid back. He was on his way to jail. With his criminal record, he was sure that it would be a while before he touched the streets again. In his mind, being in Cook County Jail was better than Burr Oaks Cemetery.

***

Nicki let her body sink into the peanut butter leather seats inside of Malaki's whip. The seat fit her body like a glove. She glanced over at him as he glided the car through the streets. His skin tone was flawless and unblemished, while his Prada button up looked good with his fitted Gucci Jeans. She was definitely turned on by the man behind the wheel. Nicki and Malaki had been talking constantly since their last date at Navy Pier. With each conversation, she was drawn further and further into his world. He was her mystery man and she was infatuated with him.

"Why are you looking at me like that?" He asked, noticing her staring at him from his peripheral vision.

"What's wrong? I can't look at you?" Nicki's tone was soft and seductive at the same time. Malaki smile, showing his pearly whites as he hopped on I-94. They were headed to Wisconsin Dells. Nicki had told Malaki that she always wanted to go there. Wisconsin Dells was in North Wisconsin and had a lot of water parks, casinos, exclusive hotels and fine restaurants. It was dead in the middle of winter so the water parks were closed. Nicki figured they could get a room at a nice hotel and have dinner at a restaurant. It didn't take much to make her happy. She just wanted to spend some quality alone time with her new friend. Malaki was happy to oblige to the small vacation. With everything that had been going on since coming to Chicago, he definitely needed some relaxation. He had a mission to accomplish in a few days with Poncho and needed some time to get his thoughts together before the hits.

"You know I never got a chance to ask. Why are you not married? You know with kids and all?" Malaki asked.

Nicki thought about the question she had just been asked before she replied.

"I don't know, I guess I don't have time for that in my life right now. Work is most important to me. Being single, I have to stay focused so these bills don't pile up." She said with a slight chuckle.

"Why you not married with kids?" Nicki asked, piggybacking off the same question Malaki just asked. "I mean you seem to have your shit together and from your conversation I can tell you are very intelligent.

"I'm like you, Nicki. I guess I don't have time." Nicki put her manicured hand on his thick hand.

"Malaki, what do you do?"

"What do you mean, what do I do?"

"I mean, you always fresh to death. You have a nice car. You must have a good job, right?"

"I'm a soldier." Malaki replied smoothly.

"Oh, you are in the army?" Nicki asked shocked.

"Yeah, or something like that."

Later that night, Malaki and Nicki were in the comfort of the Flamingo Hotel downtown Wisconsin Dells. They had spent the day shopping, went to a ski resort and ended up having dinner at the famous Pizza Pub. Nicki laid across the bed, flipping through the channels with the remote. Malaki came out the shower. Seeing Nicki's thick toned body in boy shorts cause his manhood to stiffen. He was showing a large imprint in the bath towel he had wrapped around his waist. She was gorgeous, smart and independent. Being around her always put his mind at ease. She looked so good to him. He wanted to speak but his words were caught in his throat. He wasn't used to dealing with women. His whole life had been training. Training to kill. He had never had sex and he was caught up in the moment. Nicki noticed him staring at her.

"What's good with you, soldier boy?" She asked in a joking fashion at the same time noticing Malaki's hardness under the bath towel. Malaki was embarrassed as he tried to push his 9 inches down. Nicki got up from the bed and walked over to him. Her thick thighs were jiggling with each step. Taking his chin in her small petite hands, she lifted his head and stared into his brown eyes.

"Malaki, you are so different from a lot of guys and that's why you are so special to me."

"You are beautiful to me. I like you a lot." Nicki's heart melted at Malaki's bluntness. She knew he wasn't running any type of game but speaking from the heart. She leaned in and kissed him. Their tongues explored each other's mouth. It was a lil' awkward for Malaki at first, as it was his first kiss, but he caught on quickly. He loved the feeling of Nicki's thick warm tongue in his mouth as he

118

let his hands roam over her body. Stepping away from him, Nicki removed the bath towel from Malaki's waist and couldn't believe how well he was hung. The sight of Malaki's huge shaft and huge balls made her want to cum. She had to taste him. Dropping down to her knees in front of him, she grabbed his dick with two hands. She took the head of it into her mouth while tugging on him at the same time. Nicki could taste his pre-cum on her tongue as she tried her best to deep throat him, which was impossible. Malaki was experiencing the best feeling he had ever felt. Little did he know, the best was yet to come. Nicki wasn't easy and wasn't a hoe, quick to give up the goodies, but Malaki was different and dealing with him brought the freak out of her. She sucked while at the same time jerking him off and it had Malaki going crazy. Nicki knew he was about to come by how his dick thickened. She was having none of that, she wanted him inside of her. Standing up, she pulled her tight Victoria Secret T-Shirt from over her head. She wasn't wearing a bra so her double D's were free from confinement. After pulling off her boy shorts, she laid on the bed and motioned with her index finger for Malaki to come to her. Malaki was nervous and she sensed it.

"Come here, baby. I'm not going to bite." Malaki got on the bed and was now kissing Nicki. Knowing Malaki was inexperienced, she grabbed his dick and guided it inside of her love box. Her walls gripped him tighter than the leather glove OJ Simpson put on at his trial. Nicki bit her bottom lips as Malaki's 9 inches filled her up to capacity. The warmth, wetness and tightness of Nicki's pussy was a feeling Malaki never had experienced. He thrusted inside of her with deep long strokes, breaking her walls down. Pounding inside of her, the only sounds in the room were the sounds of flesh slapping against flesh, grunts and moans. He was pleasing a woman for the first time. Nicki's nails clawed at his muscular back, drawing blood. She came over and over while Malaki felt an unfamiliar feeling coming from him.

"Ahhhhh." He moaned as he exploded thick hot nut inside of Nicki before pulling out and lying next to her. Nicki continued to plant kisses over his face and sweaty chest while smiling from ear to ear. She was falling hard and fast for the mystery man. Little did she know, he was sinking in her love just as fast.

Chapter 19

"Now, I'm going to say this one time and one time only. If you have any contraband, lighters, needles, crack pipes, matches or any drugs or narcotics, throw them in this plastic bag." The correctional officer said, throwing a black garbage bag in the middle of the floor. "Also, take your belts and shoelaces and put them in the bag. If you get caught with any of the shit I just named, best believe it ain't gonna end good for you. We are the Chicago Deputies for Cook County Jail. And for you sorry wanna be thugs, just know we're the biggest gang in muthafucker. We run this." The tall deputy informed as he smoked from the tobacco pipe in his mouth. Eight British, built officers stood beside him with black gloves covering their hands. They were no nonsense and were waiting for one of the inmates to buck, so they can enforce law with aggressive intent.

"Lil' Tony stood in a circle with at least 20 other inmates that were getting booked into Cook County Jail. This was nothing new to him. He had been going to jail since he was 13 years old and all the procedures were the same. Running the streets all his life, he knew jail came with the territory. Lil' Tony proceeded to unlace his Nike Air Max boots, throwing them in the garbage bag. He then took off his Polo belt. After tossing it in the bag, he stood back against the wall. He was being booked on Distribution of a Controlled Substance Heroin and Possession of a Firearm as a Felon. He knew his bond would be 10%. High as hell.

"Ay youngsta, if you need me to hold something until we get upstairs to the bullpen, I got you for a small fee." A dirty looking cat in a wheelchair on the side of Lil' Tony said.

"Naw, I'm cool, old school." Lil' Tony replied, eyeing the man down, who he had pegged as being a dope fiend or homeless man.

After the inmates were done throwing their contraband in the bag, the deputy retrieved the bag from the floor. The right hauling officers proceeded to strip search each inmate. The scent of must and unwashed balls invaded the air.

"Turn around, spread your cheeks, bend over and cough twice." The officer's voice boomed at Lil' Tony. He hated this part of the booking process. He always felt degraded and like less of a man. But nonetheless, he did as he was told, not wanting no smoke with the deputy. After the search, Lil' Tony put back on his clothing.

"Oh, what do we have here, old man?" Lil' Tony heard the officer say to old man in the wheelchair. The office was holding up a syringe needle in his gloved hand.

"Man, I don't know where that shit came from. Never seen that needle in my life." He lied. The needle had fell from the waistline of his dingy boxers and the officer had noticed it fall to the floor. The tall white deputy smoking the pipe came over to investigate the situation.

'You had that on this man?" He questioned the officer holding the needle.

"Sure did. Fell off his waist."

"That's a lie. He planted it on me, Sergeant." The man pleaded. The tall white officer pulled his billy club from his belt. He forcefully swung the club and connected with the man's skull, knocking him out cold. The officer swung the club four more times cracking the unconscious man's cranium. Blood splattered on Lil' Tony's Air Max boots. Blood stained the filthy floors and the sight of the man's battered skull almost made Lil' Tony throw up. The room full of inmates was so quiet you could have heard a mouse fart. The officer who had found the needle grabbed the man's wrist and checked his pulse. Feeling nothing, he looked up at the officer, who was breathing heavy from the assault he had just issued and was now putting the bloody billy club back on his belt.

"He's dead, sir." The sergeant blew smoke from his pipe.

"Welcome to Cook County Jail, ladies." He sneered.

4 hours later, Lil' Tony had completed his booking process. He had traded his street clothes in for a tan Department of Corrections jail uniform. A thick beat up mattress was under his right arm as his left hand held a pillowcase containing his County Jail care package. It consisted of a toothbrush, a bar of soap, deodorant, cheap toothpaste and a pair of shower shoes. He was headed to division 6 along with 3 other inmates. They referred to it as gladiator school.

"Four to D-6" The transition officer spoke into his walkie-talkie in front of Division 6. A few moments later, the door to the unit opened and two officers walked out and met them in the hallway. The officer that walked to other unit gave one of the guards an inmates name card. After examining the information on the cards, he gave the inmates a small pamphlet of the jail rules, before giving them their assignment.

"Tony Harman. Cell 302, second tier." Lil' Tony grabbed his copy of the jail rules and entered the unit. Cook County Jail was home to some of the most violent gangsters the city had to offer, so the tension in the jail stayed high. Walking in the dimly lit lion's den, Lil' Tony looked up to the second tier and noticed his cell was located in the corner of the tier.

"On that new!" An inmate yelled, who was sitting at a table in the dayroom playing a game of dominoes. He was letting the unit knew it was new fish on the deck. Two inmates walked up on Lil' Tony with mean mugs on their faces.

"What's good, fam? You people of folks?" He asked Lil' Tony, pertaining to his gang affiliation.

"I'm Body Snatcher!" Lil' Tony responded through clenched teeth. He pulled up his shirt, revealing the grim reaper tattoo on his chest with the words Death before Dishonor. "Your people upstairs, my nigga." The thug with the long dreads said, now knowing that Lil' Tony was official. The whole city knew about the Body Snatchers and their murderous reputation. They wanted no problems.

Lil' Tony proceeded to his cell, ice grilling the other inmates who even looked like they wanted to test his gangsta.

"God damn, my nigga. It seem like Cook County your second home, huh?" A huge man with a bald head said standing in front of cell 302, Lil' Tony's cell.

"Man, what's good, Sisco? You already know how it is in the streets. Pigs always trying to keep a gangster boxed in." Lil' Tony and Sisco gave each other a thug embrace.

'Yeah, I'm already hip. Come on in and make yourself at home. It look like we cellies."

Lil' Tony followed Sisco into the small confined cell that he would call home for God knows how long.

"What kind of beef you know?" Lil' Tony asked Sisco, throwing his mattress on the top bunk. Sisco struck a match and lit the jailhouse cigarette he had dangling between his lips.

"Punk as PO got a hold on me for a dirty urine. I should be bouncing up out of here in a minute." Sisco said blowing smoke through his nostrils.

"Aye, who them niggas posted all in front of the cell?" Lil' Tony had noticed the shiesty looking characters standing in front of the cell when he came in. Sisco looked behind him.

"Oh, you talking about fam and them? Them some lil' niggas I put down up in here. They cool."

"That's what's up."

"You already knew everybody trying to get down with us. But anyway, what's up with the big homie, Body Bag." Sisco asked, now rolling another cigarette. The question put Lil' Tony on alert.

"You know how them niggas do. They out there standing on the business," Lil' Tony replied, trying to keep it short. Leaving out the part about Body Bag having a murder contract on his head.

"I'm sorry about Ronnie too, my nigga. He was a good lil' nigga. He was starting to get to some major money I heard." Lil' Tony looked at Sisco with an intensive glare, trying to mentally read him.

"They got any word on the niggas that killed fam?" Sisco asked, throwing the cigarette in the toilet, then flushing it.

"Naw, cuz. They think it was some random niggas trying to rob him. They just caught him slipping." Lil' Tony spoke. He knew Sisco was just fishing for information. For all he knew, Sisco was the one that murdered Lil' Ronnie. He definitely wasn't trying to give Sisco any info. Sisco switched gears in the conversation.

"Well fam, I'ma let you get squared away. You already know what it is around here. You need anything, let me know."

"That's a bet." Lil' Tony proceeded to make his bed as Sisco left the cell to go and use the phone.

***

"Fuck, fuck. Beat this pussy up, nigga. Right there. Oooh, that's my spot. You hitting my spot, baby." The thick redbone moaned in ecstasy while Body Bag hit her from the back doggy style. Her ass cheeks bounced with each thrust, which only sent Body Bag more into his primal rage. His sweat glistened on his chiseled chest in the dimly lit room. The smell of sex and marijuana filled the room. Body Bag continued to pound away at her walls until he felt the feeling of his volcano about to erupt. Pulling his 9 inches from her sloppy, wet, pussy, he exploded his seed all over her back and ass crack.

"Damn shorty." He panted, slapping her as her ass cheek before collapsing on the side of her. He was spent from the work he had just put in. The redbone gave him a quick kiss on the lips before she retreated to the bathroom, giving his semi-erect dick a squeeze before climbing out the king sized bed. Body Bag watched her ass jiggle with each step as she disappeared out of the room.

"I'm definitely gonna have to keep that bitch around." He thought to himself, grabbing the half blunt of Sour Diesel Kush out the ashtray and lighting it. He inhaled the potent smoke to relax his nerves. He had a lot on his mind lately. They had to find the culprit responsible for slaying their workers, because Mr. Biggs was on his neck about it. Whoever had the balls and nerves to come at the Body Snatchers had to be crazy. The individuals who carried out the hits had to be dealt with immediately. The streets were watching and talking and if it wasn't retaliation, they would start looking like they were getting soft. The city of Chi-Raq had a lot of wolves itching and willing to take a shot at the town. Since they couldn't find the ghost responsible, they would bring the ghost to them, and when they did, they would annihilate them. In war, you had to play chess. Mental warfare was the best warfare. Destroy the mind and the body will follow.

Body Bag was taking a strong pull from the weed when his cell phone vibrated on the table beside him. Looking at the caller ID, he didn't recognize the number but nonetheless answered it.

"You have a collect call from Sisco from the Cook County Jail. To accept this call, press 1. To deny this call, press 5. To block other calls from this facility, press 7." Body Bag pressed 1, accepting the call.

"Hello."

"Yeah, what up?" Body Bag spoke with smoke in his lungs.

"I was just calling big homie to let you know that nigga Lil' Tony just pulled up on the deck."

"Oh yeah?" Body Bag sat up in bed, listening intently while the redbone slid her thick frame back under the silk sheets.

"Word. The nigga came through on a dope and pistol case. What you want us to do, boss?" Body Bag blew a thick cloud of smoke out.

"Listen and listen carefully, I need you to give him a pillow and make sure he gets some rest, feel me?"

"Say no more." Was Sisco's only reply before he hung up the telephone. The thought of Lil' Tony bleeding under a bunk caused Body Bag's dick to get hard. Lil' Tony had been on the run for months from the Body Snatchers but in the end, the point would be made. You can't run from the Body Snatchers. The redbone saw Body Bag's wood stand like the Eiffel Tower and stepped to her business. Feeling her mouth wet his pole, he grabbed the back of her head, making her take all of him. In the end, it would all come together and all his enemies would be laid to rest.

Chapter 20

"If we can manage to get inside the warehouse, we might be able to catch Mr. Biggs in there and send him to his maker." Poncho informed Malaki as they sat in his living room going over the war plans they were about to execute.

"So, if we can't catch this Mr. Biggs character, what's the next step, Poncho?"

"If we cannot catch him there, we will continue to keep eliminating the people in the black book. The more of them we kill, the more we will dismantle his organization and we will eventually bring him out of hiding, Eśey."

"I just don't understand how killing these people have anything to do with the death of my parents." Malaki was confused. He had come to Chicago for one reason and one reason only. To kill Mr. Biggs and the detective responsible for his father's death. Taking care of the detective had given him a breath of fresh air, but the weight of Mr. Biggs remained heavy on his mind. Only the death of Mr. Biggs could put his mind at ease.

"Malaki, what do you know about war?" Poncho said, standing up clasping his hands behind his back.

"I probably know the same things you know about war."

"No, no, my friend." Poncho waved his finger in the air for emphasis.

"In my country, war is a way of life. We are taught at a very early age of the politics at war. That is something you must learn." Malaki let out a slight chuckle.

"In case you didn't know, my friend, I was trained by one of the best Special OPs commanders in the United States Army. He didn't train me in politics, I was trained in killing."

"This American Special OPs man you speak so highly of, I never heard of him. I'm quite sure you have heard of the Madina Cartel. That is who I represent and that is who I work for."

"And you tell me this to say what?" Malaki replied taking offense to what Poncho was saying.

"My friend, no need to deal with feelings. We are on the same side and battlefield. I was just trying to get you to see the importance of mental warfare. I understand your situation and as for your parents, I also feel your pain. I too have lost my parents and had to deal with grief, but trust and believe, this Mr. Biggs will get what he has coming for the pain he has caused you. My boss sent me here to kill him, and that's what I plan to do. He is good at hiding out. He knows my boss has issued his death warrant. I have been in this city for almost a year now and have not yet found the hole he resides in." Malaki nodded his head in understanding. He hadn't found the logic in Poncho's strategy but at the same time found Poncho was sincere at motivated.

"Poncho, I just want this man dead as soon as possible, that's all. You are right. We are fighting the same enemy and his blood must be shed at all cost. We are on the same team so let's make it happen." Poncho smiled at Malaki and extended his hand. The two men shook hands, putting their differences aside. They both had one common interest that bonds them and that was murdering Mr. Biggs and anything or anyone that stood in their way.

"So, tell me, how we are going to get in the warehouse?" Malaki asked now, back on the strategic planning of Mr. Biggs' demise.

"The warehouse is located on the Westside of the city. It said that they sell a lot of drugs out of that building and it brings in less than 500,000 each and every week. If we can bring that building down, we will put a hell of a dent in Mr. Biggs pockets. Hopefully, he will be there when we do it and we can put an end to this." Malaki sat and thought about what Poncho was saying and it didn't sit right with him. Malaki had since clicking up with Poncho played follow the leader. Now, it was time for him to man up and take charge.

"Poncho, I have a better way we can take down the building."

"So, how do you think we should take down the building?" Poncho said with interest.

"Remember these rifles you showed me back when we first met?"

"Of course."

128

"I think it's time I really show you what I specialize in, Poncho." Malaki continued to lay down his murderous plan to Poncho. It was now time to bring pure terror to the city.

Body Bag sat in the comfort of his new Bentley Bentayga SUV, sipping on a bottle of Hennessy. He was parked in the back of the 2 Amigos Body Shop on Western Street, waiting for Killa Fred to pull up. Killa had told him he needed to meet with him to discuss some serious business, so Body Bag told him to meet him at the body shop. It was 12:00 in the day as the thick snowflakes began to fall over the City of Chi. The murder rate in the city had began to rise and Body Bag and his crew of murderers had played a major part in the bloodshed. Murder was second nature to him and his blood thirst made him a feared man. Body Bag lived by the code of the late Niccolo Mackeceli. He would rather be feared than loved, because in his murderous mind, love changed but fear would forever be instilled in those who went against the grain.

Looking at his Breguet La Marine timepiece surrounding his wrist, the time read 12:15. A smile came across his lips as he watched the hand tick on the watch he paid 90,000 dollars for. He noticed that Killa Fred was running a lil' late and was about to call him, until he saw the Aston Martin Vantage pull in the back of the body shop. Hitting the push button on the dashboard, the engine to the Bentley became silent. Body Bag took one last swig from the Hennessy bottle before he hopped out the whip as Killa Fred was pulling up next to the expensive SUV. Body Bag pulled the hoodie on his quarter length mink coat over his head to protect him from the blistering Chicago wind. After hitting the button on his key chain and locking the door, he jumped in the Aston with his boss.

"What's good, Killa?" He greeted once in the whip.

"Same ol' shit. Murda and money." Killa Fred replied shaking hands with his young protégé.

Putting the car in drive, Killa Fred pulled out of the lot of the body shop. Glancing over at Body Bag, Killa Fred asked, "What's the deal with G them, nigga?"

"I'm in this process of baking them niggas a cake as we speak."

Killa Fred raised his eyebrow. "Well, I'm listening." Killa Fred grabbed the freshly rolled blunt of Kush and sparked it.

"The way I see it, fam, is these niggas got some kind of information on the location of our most lucrative spots in the city. They been hitting everything and killing our workers. Some time they take the money and drugs and sometimes they don't take shit."

Killa Fred took a strong pull from the blunt. "Where do you think they get the information from?"

"That's what I can't figure out." Body Bag replied, grabbing the blunt from Killa Fred.

"So, what's the plan, youngsta?"

"Since we can't find them, we gon' bring them to us. You know the White House is our spot out west. It's the warehouse. I got a plan that's gonna bring some major attention to it. As you remember before we slumped shorty, he said one of the cats was black, the other one was Mexican. So, we gone be on point. First Mexican we see, we gone snatch his ass up and see what's up with him and go from there." Body Bag took a strong pull of the blunt and passed it back.

"Y'all just make sure to get this situation over with because the boss is on my back about this."

"I got you, big homie. Oh yeah, before I forget, we found Lil' Tony."

"Is that right?"

"Yeah. He ended up in Cook County Jail. He on Division 6."

"We got any soldiers in there on that deck?"

"Aint no secret." Body Bag retorted.

"Make sure you get taken care of." Killa Fred said pulling back behind the body shop.

"I'm already on it, Killa."

"Good. That's what I like to hear. Once, we get this shit done and over with, we can get back to the money."

"Don't even trip, boss. You already know I'm on the job." Body Bag replied getting out the car and jumping in his whip with one thing on his mind. Murda Murda!

Lil' Tony sat at the small desk inside the cell, writing a letter to his aunt in an attempt to get some bond money. His bond was $3,000 and at 10% all he had to do was come up with $300 . He didn't have a red penny to his name. The police had confiscated his cash he had in his pocket saying that it was drug money. He wasn't scheduled for court for another month and he had to get out of Cook County as soon as possible. He knew he was on dangerous grounds. Lil' Tony prayed that his aunt Donnie would help him out by posting his bond. If not, he would surely have to wait till his next court appearance. Lil' Tony was startled when Sisco and two other inmates walked in the cell.

"What's up? Y'all need to get up in here?" Lil' Tony asked ready to give his celly some privacy.

"Nah, you good, scud. We just about to smoke this joint real quick. You trying to smoke?" Sisco asked while one of the men that accompanied him pulled out a fat joint and used a match to light it.

"Yeah, thats cool." Lil' Tony replied, not wanting to miss a chance at getting high for free. The thug that lit the weed took a strong pull from the joint before passing it to Lil' Tony. Taking a drag from the joint and inhaling the smoke, Lil' Tony felt the effects from the THC immediately enter his bloodstream.

"This some good shit, my nigga. Who got this for sale?" Lil' Tony asked passing the joint to the next man in rotation.

"This shit came from Division 2. I can put an order in for you if you want." Sisco said accepting the weed from his celly.

'Yeah, I might. I'ma let you know. One of the men that came in the cell with Sisco looked out the cell trying to spot any sign of a Correctional Officer. Seeing no one, the man nodded at Sisco. Lil' Tony thought he was just paranoid from his high as he was noticing the strange movements from the men in the cell.

"Aye fam, I got a message for you." Sisco pulled a 9 inch rusty jailhouse shank from off his waist. At the sight of the monstrous weapon in Sisco's hand, Lil' Tony now knew he was in immediate danger. His heartbeat stopped.

"What's this all about?" He stuttered at the same time passing gas. He knew he was dead as a doorknob. Everything seemed to move in slow motion as one of the men rushed Lil' Tony, punching him in his jaw. It broke on impact, knocking him to the floor.

"The message, my nigga, is to never steal from the Body Snatchers and think your actions will go unpunished!" Sisco sneered before he stuck the rusty steel inside Lil' Tony's stomach. The cold piercing steel went into his flesh like it was melted butter. The smell of fresh blood and shit filled the cell from Lil' Tony losing his bowels from facing death. Lil' Tony's screams fell on the ears of the rest of the inmate on the unit. His horrific pleas for help were frivolous as everybody continued to mind their own business. To them, it was just another day in Cook County Jail

"Stand his bitch ass up!" Sisco commanded with his clothes soiled with Lil' Tony's blood. The goons did as they were told. Lil' Tony had no more fight from the massive loss of blood. The three killers took Lil' Tony's weak body out the cell and aligned his body over the top tier. His body landed on a table in the dayroom where four Mexicans were playing a game of spades. The Mexicans calmly got up from the table and walked in opposite directions. Officer Johnson was in the guard station when she saw the bloody body bounce off the table and hit the body alarm.

"All inmates step in a cell and lock down. I repeat lockdown. Lockdown."

The deputies rushed the unit in riot gear in attempts to secure the inmates in their cells. Sisco ditched the bloody knife in a nearby trash can as he watched the officers load Lil' Tony's lifeless body on a stretcher. His eyes were still open as his pulse was gone. He was given to the grim reaper. Sisco knew after they did the investigation and rewound the cameras, he would be picked up for the assault. He had come in Cook County Jail for a minor parole violation and would now be charged with a murder. His future would be given to the Statesville Penitentiary for life. In his mind, it all came with the territory of being affiliated with the infamous Body Snatcher Organization.

Chapter 21

"So, you really think you can drop a body from that far away? I mean that's almost 6 city blocks, compadre."

"Poncho, trust and believe that I can make the shot. You just make sure you handle your end and clean up the mess." Malaki replied as he wiped the barrel of the 30.06 down with WD-40. The two were in a secluded location about to head to the warehouse on the deep Westside to lay the murder game. The plan was simple. A message had to be sent to Mr. Biggs and the Body Snatchers that everybody at the warehouse would have to be shot and killed. Malaki would use the rifle to dismantle the gang's security and once the security was left without their soul, Poncho would proceed inside of the building. He would kill any and everything is his way. Hopefully, he'd murder Mr. Biggs in the process.

"Don't worry, my friend. You just knock down the men on the outside and let me handle the rest. I will drop you off at the building." Poncho pointed to a spot on the mop that was laid across the table." From here, you should be able to make the shot undetected." Malaki was now screwing the silencer on the rifles threaded barrel. Poncho went under the cushion of the couch to retrieve the two fully automatic Glock 17 with 50 shot drums attached to them. After the two assassins were locked and loaded down with ammunition, they made their way to the stolen van that was parked behind the building. They had one thing on their mind and that was the bodies they were about to catch and the family's they were about to leave to mourn.

Thirty minutes later, Poncho pulled the van behind an alley and parked. Looking at his watch, the time read 6:15.

"Listen, my friend, at 6:30 you start taking care of the business. If everything goes as planned, I will meet you back here at this location. If not, you already know the business. Oh before I go, put this number in your phone. If I don't make it back, call this number it belongs to my boss. Let him know I served him to the best of my ability." Poncho stored the number in Malaki's phone.

"Don't worry, Poncho. Everything will be all well. Now, let's get active," was Malakis only reply. He slid on a pair of Nike baseball gloves. Pulling his black ski-mask over his face, he grabbed his rifle and exited the vehicle on a mission to kill his opposition.

"Make sure you keep this line moving!" Body Bag commanded, referring to the line of dope fiends that stood impatiently in line. They were waiting to get served the best heroin the city had to offer. Body Bag had devised a plan that would bring some major attention to the warehouse by offering and promoting free bags of dope for a 24 hour shift. He knew that every dope fiend in the city of Chicago would be at The White House. Body Bag was hoping and praying that the mysterious killers that had been killing their workers would try and pull over. And when they did, his man would be on point. Body Bag stood in front of the line of fiends, playing the part of the soldier that he was. He dressed in dark green army fatigue pants and a black hoodie. A Draco AK-47 hung from a sling on his neck like a chain. The mini assault rifle's banana clip was loaded with 30 rounds of 7.62 armor piercing bullets.

Security was set up tight around the warehouse. Two men with AR-15's paced the roof of the building as four soldiers stood posted in the front securing the dope line. Each man was clutching some kind of automatic weapon. A black Cadillac Escalade was parked on the side of the building. Sitting in the confines of the SUV, two armed men sat smoking a blunt of loud with pistols laid across their laps.

Poncho blended in well in the sea of dope fiends. His dirty looking dreads fell down his back while the dirty trench coat he wore looked like he had found it at the bottom of a dumpster. The man behind him began to vomit. He was apparently sick from not having his daily dose of heroin. Mother Heroin was a physical beast that demanded attention, and if ignored, could cause hellacious symptoms. Poncho began to get closer and closer to the front of the line as his sweaty palms gripped the plastic Glocks that rested beneath his trench coat. Looking at the man in front of the line barking orders, Poncho's photographic memory kicked in. He wouldn't believe his eyes or his luck. Standing before him was a trophy piece.

The murderous Body Bag. A sneer came across Poncho's lips at the thought of putting Body Bag's brains on the pavement. He knew that Body Bag was a designated hitter for Mr. Biggs and the Body Snatchers. This alone let him know that he was getting closer and closer to Mr. Biggs.

Malaki was in an abandoned building. His rifle hanging discreetly out a broken window as he looked through the lens of the optic scope that rested on top of the rifle. His finger rested inside the trigger guard slightly covering the cold trigger with a gloved hand. He was approximately 6 blocks away from the warehouse so he calculated that his shots would be at least 1,950 feet away. He knew that his accuracy was on point as he had made shots of 2,500 feet. Through the scope, Malaki scanned the premises of the warehouse. He noticed the two men on the top of the building with rifles. He did not know if these men were accurate with their weapons as he deemed them as a security threat. He chose to eliminate them first. Placing the butt of the rifle to his right shoulder, Malaki focused his pain on one of the men. Adjusting the expensive scope, he lined the crosshairs on the middle of the man's chest. The individual who seemed to be smoking a cigarette was only 18 years old and had been recruited by the Body Snatcher's only 3 months prior. Malaki controlled his breathing as he applied a slow and steady squeeze to the trigger.

Foooth.

The gunshot sounded like a car door being closed as the lead slow traveled through the air at the speed of sound, slamming into the man's chest and blowing his heart out. He felt nothing as his body fell and blood poured from the large hole in his back. Malaki pulled the slide back on the rifle ejecting the hot shell casing that had just caused death.

"Aye, my nigga. Say, its gone be crackin' at the pub tonight. You trying to slide through?" AJ said as he rounded the top of the building, only to see his potna on his back. AJ attempted to grab his walkie talkie.

Foooth.

The slug found home in his cranium. His brains were melted and knocked out the back of his head in a pinkish mist. Malaki pulled the trigger again hitting him in the chest for good measure before his body dropped. Now that he eliminated his targets on the top of the warehouse, he focused his attention on the tinted SUV. From his view, he focused the rifle's scope on the front windshield and squeezed

Foooth. Foooth.

The man behind the wheel was about to pass the blunt to his mans until hot led punctured his face, killing him instantly. The passenger screamed in horror from the site of half his guy's face missing. The smell of blood caused him to gag as he reached for the door handle. Jumping out of the truck, he made a vague attempt to run.

Foooth.

He fell face first on the cold concrete from being shot in the back of the head. Malaki's emotions were numb while he reloaded his weapon.

Poncho was now third in line and it was time to get active. He was staring at Body Bag. He was about to pull his Glocks until he heard a piercing scream and all hell broke out. The fiends all took off in different directions.

Scanning to see his surroundings, Poncho saw a body sprawled out on the pavement. Three armed men stood by the body. One of them was on a walkie talkie. Pulling his twin glocks, he turned his attention back to Body Bag, who now had the Draco in his hands. They locked eyes for what seemed like an eternity before triggers were pulled. Poncho heard the loud AK bark as he pulled his trigger. Both men missed. Body Bag took cover behind a dumpster and continued to let the Draco speak while Poncho hid behind an abandoned car. Poncho released a fury of shots at Body Bag.

Malaki saw the drama through the lens of his scope. He had to get Poncho out of the tight situation he was in. The three remaining security guys fired their weapons with malicious intent, trying to end Poncho's life. Malaki placed his cross hair on the man's throat and squeezed. The man grabbed at his throat in an attempt to stop the blood from pouring from the wound .He was in shock. The next guy fired his weapon at Poncho until his 30 round magazine was now empty.

"Fuck!" He cursed in frustration. Malaki now had another gunner in his deadly scope

Footh!

He released another round, knocking the man head off, splattering blood and brain tissue on the man next to him. He was met with the same fate, also getting a bullet to the head.

Boc, Boc, Boc.

"Come out with your hands up, Migo." Poncho spoke. He knew that Body Bag was out of bullets.

Body Bag tossed his empty rifle to the ground. He had no win. "What the fuck do you all want?"

"We went to know the whereabouts to your boss."

Boc.

"I don't know what you are talking about." Body Bag lied. Poncho placed a fresh clip in the glock.

"Listen amigo, I just want to talk to you. I want to offer you a proposition."

"What if I refuse?"

"Then, you die." Body Bag thought about his current situation. He was a killa to say the least but now he was on the other side of the gun. He had come to the terms that he wasn't ready to die. He now knew he was up against some real killers. Body Bag stepped from behind the dumpster with his hands above his head. Poncho smiled, before he walked up to Body Bag with his Glocks extended. "You make good choice, Eśey," was all he said before he smashed one of the glocks against Body Bag's skull, knocking him out cold. Malaki had just finished dissembling the rifle and wiping off his prints throughout the vacant building that he may have touched when Poncho pulled in to the alley behind the building. Once Malaki got in the barn, he saw a bloodied Body Bag who was zip tied at his wrist and ankle, preventing him from escape. Malaki had saw the whole ordeal through his scope.

"Why didn't you kill him?" Malaki asked, nodding at the unconscious Body Bag. Poncho put the van in drive and pulled out of the alley.

"Because Eśey, he is going to tell us where Mr. Biggs is."

"What if he doesn't?"

"Oh, trust and believe, my friend. He will tell us everything that we want to know." Poncho informed.

An hour later, Poncho pulled the van into a wooded area. It was dark and the snow had just begun to fall. Malaki was anxious to know where they were headed.

"Where are we going, Poncho?"

"Don't worry, my friend. We are here." Poncho pulled up to a farmhouse. The house seemed to be deserted and unoccupied.

"Who lives here?" Poncho ignored Malaki's minor investigation and turned the ignition off. Opening the side door to the van, Poncho pulled a rag out of his pocket and used a Visine bottle to squirt liquid on it before putting it to Body Bag's nose. He instantly squirmed out of his slight coma.

"Wake up, sleepy head." Poncho slapped Body Bag across his face to make sure he was fully awake. He pulled him out of the van and tossed him over his shoulder. Looking at Malaki, he said, "Follow me, heffa!" Malaki followed Poncho to the back of the farmhouse to a barn behind the house. Once in the barn, Poncho laid Body Bag's body on the ground and kicked him in his ribs, cracking one in the process, Body Bag knew he was in a deadly situation and his chance of making it out alive was slim to none. Poncho pulled a string that was hanging from the ceiling and light invaded the inside of the dark barn. Malaki looked around the dimly lit barn. It was almost completely empty except for the huge steel drum that sat in the middle. The barn had a funny smell that he had gotten familiar with since coming to Chicago. The smell was death.

Poncho grabbed Body Bag by his leg and drug him to the side of the large steel drum. Body Bags pleas for money were muffled, due to the grey electric tape that covered his mouth.

"Poncho, what are you doing?"

"Malaki, my friend, you must learn to just go with the flow. I'm going to show you a trick, my friend that will always get information from somebody." Poncho said as he pushed a button on the side of the wall. At that moment, a thick chain descended down from a cable coming from the roof. "Malaki, let me tell you a little story. A story about my uncle His name was Santago El' Maro. At the age of 19, he worked for a cartel as a full time operative. These deadly men were at war with another cartel and the bodies were piling up at a rapid rate. The family my uncle worked for needed a new way or method to dispose of the bodies of their enemies. Until then, they just dumped the shot up bodies in the sewers or the city's river. That was risky for the cartel so they employed a chemist from Israel, who taught them how to dissolve corpses in acid." Poncho tied the chain to Body Bags feet and then continued the story. "My uncle used large drums like this. We call them oil drums where I'm from. He got Caustic soda that he bought from hardware store for $1.50 He used a hundred pounds of powder to dissolve one human corpse. He always told me that he never cut up the bodies but dumped them in the oil drum complete. I saw my uncle do this numerous times throughout my life. You know, Malaki, my uncle confessed to the Mexican government that he was responsible for dissolving over 300 bodies. At one point, he was disposing over 30 a month. They sentenced him to life in Federal Prison. In the newspaper, they named him the Stew Maker." Poncho said then let out a satanic chuckle before he snatched the electric tape from Body Bag's mouth.

After hearing the murderous story, he knew he wasn't in the company of any ordinary street niggas. The men standing before him was in a league of their own.

Poncho pushed a button on the wall and the chain began to move, pulling Body Bags body up into the air until he was hanging directly over the oil drum that was filled with the deadly Caustic Soda. "Come on. Please, don't kill me."

"Shut up, puta. Now, I'm going to ask you a very important question. How you answer this question will determine how you

die. Do you understand?" Poncho's demand was direct and asser-
tive. Body Bag's killer, homicidal demeanor was gone and now replaced by a regular civilian, knowing they were about to be murdered by his opposition. He had played the game of the streets and
lost. For all the murders he committed since a youngster, he failed
to adhere to the law of the land. Live by it, die by it. Not wanting to
die a horrific death, he proceeded to tell Poncho and Malaki the information they needed. Malaki logged the information in his iPhone.

"You are not lying to me, are you?" Poncho interrogated.

"No, man. I swear." Body Bag replied. Poncho pressed the button and Body Bags body was lowered into the oil drum. A quarter
of his head made contact with the cinnamon smelling liquid before
Poncho hit the button again, pulling him back up. A few seconds
later, Body Bag started to feel a burning sensation at the top of his
cap. His head started smoking and he smelled the sickening smell
of burning human flesh.

"Ahhhh!" His scream was diabolical.

"Now, I'm going to ask you. Are you telling me the truth?"
Body Bag tried to reply as he felt his skin melting on the side of his
face. Malaki had to turn his head from the gruesome site before him.
Feeling that his enemy wasn't being truthful, Poncho pushed the
button on the wall again. He lowered Body Bag's body into the oil-
drum completely while looking at his watch. Two minutes had
passed by. He pushed the button on the wall again, pulling it out of
the oil-drum. Body Bag's corpse had vanished into the afterlife
along with his howl. Malaki knew now that he was in the presence
of Lucifer himself. The world was a corrupt and violent place. You
had killas, you had murderers, and you had goons but Poncho was
a monsta.

Chapter 22

Castilino Madina sat at his large oak desk inside his mansion outside of Juarez, Mexico. He had just gotten off the phone and the disturbing news he had just received was devastating. He had just found out that his only daughter, Grace Madina, was missing. She was to have returned from Tiajuana the night before. A note had been left at her hotel. The note read.

Bow down to the new regime.

Castilino's chest was in his back as he thought about his beautiful daughter in the hands of his merciless enemies. The Los Teccas. Born in Laredo, Texas in 1970 to two hard working farmers, Castilino's parents did everything to raise their only son right. Castilino was big for his size, securing him a linebacker position on Laredo United High School's football team. Castilino embraced his high school popularity and was a regular at the Laredo party scene. At the age of 19, Castilino had his first encounter with the law when he was arrested for running down a middle school counselor with his truck while driving drunk. He was charged with Negligent Homicide. However, he was never sentenced for the felony act.

Getting tired of the normal life of a young man, he was influenced by and looked up to the Narcos of the the drug trade. Castilino fled to Mexico and joined the Boro Cartel. Castilino quickly climbed the ranks and become the head of the assassins. He finally became head of the Cartel's operating in Acapulco. As head of operations, he led the Cartel' s efforts to invade over Nuevo Laredo, home and territory of the Los Teccas Cartel, a murderous cartel led by the infamous "El Chico." With a thirst for power, Castilino sanctioned the murder of El Boro, leader and Chief of the Boro Cartel. Taking his seat at the throne, The Boro was now under new management. It was renamed the Madina Cartel and Castilino was the Boss of all Bosses.

At the height of his power, Castilino needed an easier way to bring his heroin and cocaine into the United States. A raid on his home from Mexican authorities revealed automatic weapons, grenades and police uniforms. His name was added to the most wanted list on both sides of the border and a 4 million dollar bounty was placed on his head.

"Seeing Tijuana as his only option to transport his drugs into the states, he offered to pay the Los Tecca Cartel handsomely to allow passage through Tijuana. El Chico allowed the Madina Cartel's semi-trucks loaded with Narcotics to pass through Tijuana and into Laredo Texas until El Chico's greed made him go up on the passage fee. Castilino's trucks were now getting pulled over and his drugs were being confiscated. He refused to pay the new passing price and instead, sent a squad of assassins to kill 9 police officials. He hung their naked bodies under an overpass. That act of power sparked a war between the Cartels that had been forever lasting with casualties on both sides.

Castilino stood up from his desk and began to pace back and forward. How could he be so stupid? He thought to his self. When Grace asked him could she visit Tijuana to attend her friend's wedding, he had told her that she couldn't go, due to the conflict with the Los Teccas. He should've known that Grace would oblige to his orders and for that reason, he should've placed security on her to prevent her from leaving the estate. It was times like the Castilino knew his wife was looking down at him from the heavens above and shaming him for his lack of firmness on their beloved daughter. Castilino stared out the window into a sea of his acres of loud. He knew that the Los Teccas would not show mercy on his seed's head. He caused them too much blood and grief. He needed Poncho immediately if he had any chance at getting Grace back and out of harm's reach. He dialed Poncho's number only to get the voicemail of the young assassin. Cursing himself in visible frustration, he turned to his bodyguard Gonzalez, who stood silently against the wall. He was holding an AR-15 awaiting his boss's instructions.

"I don't care what you have to do. Get my daughter back. Vominos! Do not come back to her without her. Do you hear me? If you come back to her without my child, I will have you cut up in pieces and your body will be found all over Mexico!" Castilino yelled as his tears stained his cheeks. He was losing it in front of his man. At a time when he was supposed to show immaculate strength, he was showing obvious weakness. His bodyguard let his distraught boss vent and release his emotions. Gonzalez nodded his head in understanding, acknowledging his boss orders and left the room. Castilino sat at his desk and reached for the bottle of 1800 Tequila and twisted the top off. After taking a long swig from the bottle, the smooth liquid seemed to warm his chest as the liquor began to float through his bloodstream. Mentally, he tried to assess his situation as well as his enemy. El Chico was a war lord with ambition to be the number one most feared cartel boss in the world. The history of his adversary was treacherous.

El Chico's main line of business was kidnapping. He lived by the motto that criminals earn respect and credibility with creative killing methods. He believed that your status is based on your capacity to commit the most sadistic acts of murder. Burning corpses using acid and beheading his victims set a new generation of savagery. One of El Chico's lieutenants went by the name of Crutches for the trail of disabled people he left behind him. El Chico and his cartel of murderers didn't believe in dissolving the bodies at their victims. It is a fact that the corpse of a few of his own men were dumped on Rosarito Beach with their tongues cut out. It was a warning to others that were accused of snitching to the police about cartel business. In another incident, 15 decapitated heads were found in a large garbage bag outside of Tijuana. They were said to be the heads of men and women who owed small drug debts to the Los Teccas. El Chico adopted the evil killing tactic and idea from the beheadings in Iraq. The Mexican government could do little with El Chico and his cartel. He instilled fear in even the FEDS, who were afraid to put his photos on their wanted list in case he retaliated against them.

Castilino knew that his arch enemy was a force to be beefing with, but with his daughters life at stake, he was willing to cash in all of his chips and come at El Chico and the Los Teccas with all that he had. If his life would be the cost, then so be it. The war with the Los Teccas had been bloody to the core, but Castilino was about to turn the volume up. His body count was about to flourish into something devilish.

Grace Madina sat on a couch inside a locked room somewhere in Mexico. She was hungry, cold and scared to death. She didn't know where she was because after being tossed in the SUV, a pillowcase was put over her head. Grace knew that she should've listened to her father when he told he not to go into Tijuana. Her friend Ann was getting married and a party was being held after the wedding. She wouldn't miss it if she wanted. After her mother was murdered when she was the tender age of 12, her father had been overly protective of her. She felt the 10 million dollar mansion she resided in was nothing but a maximum security prison. On the way to Tijuana, she sat in the backseat of the cab feeling guilty. She knew that her father would feel some kind of way about her sneaking out of the house and disobeying his authority. She knew that he didn't deserve that but at the same time, she was young and wanted to live her life. Grace figured she could go out, have a good time and be back before her father knew that she was gone. She was wrong.

Grace was at the after party doing a little drinking and smoking weed. Going in the Chanel bag, she grabbed her Newport box and saw that she was out of cigarettes. She asked one of the guys who attended the party that she knew named Hector to take her to the gas station to get some smokes. He agreed and they got in his Ford pickup truck. They made the five minute drive to the Pamex Gas Station. After purchasing her box of Newport's, Grace got back in the truck. Hector was about to pull out of the gas station until two black SUV's pulled into the parking lot, boxing him in. The doors to the vehicles swung open and two masked men hopped out, pointing large semi-automatic handguns. One of the men opened the driver side door and yanked Hector out of the driver seat. After forcing him to the pavement, the gunman put the gun to Hector's head and squeezed the trigger five times. That put his brains on the concrete. Grace jumped at the loud sound of the .40 caliber weapons before she let out a deafening scream. The second gunman snatched her door open and punched her in the jaw. They snatched her out of the truck with extreme aggression and at gunpoint forced her into the SUV. The truck sped out of the gas station leaving a kidnapping and homicide for the police investigate.

Walking over to the bedroom door, Grace tried to turn the knob. It was locked. She could hear voices on the other side of the door speaking Spanish. She began to bang on the door. After a few moments, she could hear keys before the door was opened. A large man holding a brown bag entered the room and tossed her the bag. The inside of the bag contains an apple, two tortillas and a plastic bag filled with some cold ground beef.

"Please, I want to go home." Grace pleaded letting the brown paper bag hit the floor. The large man looked at the features of Grace's exotic beautiful face, down to her young ample breast and fixed his perverted gaze on the exposed brown thick thighs. He started to get aroused as his dick began to swell inside his tight wrangler jeans. He gave his meat a squeeze before he turned and closed the door. "Please, just leave me alone." Grace said. Looking at the room for any way to escape, she found none. The room she was in had no windows. It was one way in, one way out. She had nowhere to run.

"Come on, mamacita! Don't make me have to take it." The bodyguard shot, advancing toward Grace. She was backed up against the wall as the 300 pound beast invaded her personal space. The musty and sour smell coming off his body almost made her throw up, as he attempted to kiss her. Grace wasn't going out without a fight and used her manicured nails to claw at his face.

"Ahhhh!" The bodyguard yelled in agony before he back slapped Grace in the face, splitting her lip on contact. "You puta. Now I'm going to show you some respect." He grabbed her by the throat with his massive hand and with the other one, began to unbuckle his diamond studded belt buckle. He pulled his pants down as he freed his rigid penis that oozed of pre-cum. Tossing her on the bed with brute force, he climbed on top of her. He pinned her hands above her head while he savagely began to suck on one of her exposed nipples. Tears ran down Grace's face when she felt her satin panties ripped off of her. She tried to fight the monster off of her but her struggle was futile.

"Get off of her!" She heard a voice command. She saw a figure standing in the doorway. He was dressed from head to toe in Army fatigue as an assault weapon hung from his right shoulder. The enraged bodyguard looked back to see who had killed his moment. Seeing who it was, he immediately got up and pulled up his pants.

"My apologies, Senor." The man walked up to the bodyguard, getting in his face.

"Your job is to make sure this room is secured. If you can't handle your duties and do as you're told, I'm quite sure we can find you another occupation. Maybe digging graves, si?"

"No, El Senor."

"Get out of here!" The man said grabbing the bodyguard by the collar of his shirt and forcefully pushing him out the door. Turning back to Grace, who sat on the bed with her knees to her chest, he told her. "Eat your lunch. It is all you will have for the next 3 hours."

"What do you want with me?" The man stared at her, admiring her beauty before he answer that question.

"100 million from your father. He pay, you live. He not pay, you die." Grace put her head down. She now knew whose hands her life laid in. It was in the Los Teccas and her chances of making it out alive were slim to none.

Arturo closed the door behind him and locked it, leaving his hostage in the confines of the small bedroom. Grabbing his cell phone from his front pocket, he placed a call to his boss. The phone rang three times before El Chico answered.

"Como estas."

"Como estas, El Jefe. How much longer?"

"We are still waiting. You more than anybody know that these things cannot be rushed, Arturo. Patience is a virtue. He is on our time and when the time on the clock runs outs, you know what to do. Comprende?"

"Si, Senor." was Arturo's only reply before he ended the call. He was beginning to become frustrated with the current situation. This wasn't his first kidnap ransom. He did this for a living but something about the girl in the room was different them the rest of his past victims. It was something he felt that he couldn't explain.

Born in 1976 in a small village in Southern Mexico, Arturo joined the army to escape poverty. He wanted to join the elite

GAFE, Mexico's equivalent to the United States Green Berets. He trained with Israeli Defense forces at the infamous school of the American in Georgia and then at Fort Bragg in North Carolina, home to the United States Army Special Forces. Back in Mexico, Arturo used what they had been taught to suppress the Zappatista, largely indigenous Mayon protesting about the poverty of their people. Armed with only .22 caliber rifle, they fled from their regular army base. By the time Arturo and his team caught up with them at the edge of the jungle. Within hours, 34 Zapatistas were dead. The Zaposista leadership was also gunned down and murdered by Arturo and his machine gun crew. Their corpses were found on a riverbank with their ears and noses cut off.

Sent north to the border, Arturo discovered the garish mansions of the cartel bosses, all night parties and fell in love with the party life and prostitutes. It was a major change from the mud and heat of the jungle. As Mexico moved forward and was more open democracy, Arturo ended up meeting El Chico at a local bar in Tijuana. Arturo told El Chico about his military history, which only intrigued El Chico. El Chico offered Arturo a prominent position with the Los Tecca's after his background was confirmed. Arturo was officially a part of the Los Tecca Cartel as an operative field general after completing several murder contracts in Tijuana law enforcement. Artuor's killing tactics and strategic moves got him promoted to second in command in the Los Tecca's organization. The rumors was that Arturo and his crew of henchman participated or sanctioned the deaths of more than 1,000 people. The kidnapping of Castilino Madina's daughter was easy to say the least as the Los Teccas had eyes everywhere. 100 million US dollars was a small price to pay for such a beautiful woman. Arturo thought to himself. He was intoxicated by her beauty. He knew his boss and the heat that he had for Castilino. It had been too much bloodshed. It was no doubt in his mind that El Chico would order the execution of Grace, even if Castilino paid the ransom. It was an act for war and supremacy in the eyes of El Chico. Arturo knew that it was just business but the feeling he was starting to have for Grace was something personal. He didn't know if he could just sit back and let her innocence and life be taken away from her. She did not deserve it. As of right now, he would just play it by ear and see how everything went. Looking at his watch, he saw it was 7:15. In another 3 hours it would be time to feed the hostage again. When the time came, he would deliver her bag lunch personally. He wanted a little time with her alone. If only for just a few minutes.

2 Days Later

Gonzalez sat in the passenger seat of a tinted Yukon Denali. Three other men occupied the truck. The men were sitting outside of a two story home in Tijuana, Baja California. The home belonged to Alfredo Arteaga AKA El Agrigun. He was a Los Tecca operative, whose brother was Municipal Police officer, who was also the head of security. Thus, making him a part of the Los Tecca Cartel. Castilino wanted all associated with the Los Teccas and the organization to be laid to rest. He would stop at nothing until his daughter was returned to him unharmed. Castilino still had not contacted Poncho as he knew the assassin had his hands full in Chicago, trying to serve Mr. Biggs his death warrant. Gonzalez would have to take his place.

"Gonzales slid the 30 round magazines inside the butt of his MP5 submachine gun. The only sound audible inside of the SUV was the sound of clips being inserted into high profile arms and live rounds being injected into the chambers of fully automatics. Gonzales glanced at his watch. It was now time to kill. It was late at night and he figured nobody would see it coming or leaving the house. Pulling his ski mask over his face, he got out of the vehicle as his henchman followed suit. Stealthily, the men made their way up the driveway ready to home invade and cause massive homicide.

Sitting at the dinner table reading a copy of the Tijuana newspaper, Alfredo waited for his wife of 35 years to serve dinner. Tonight, she was making his favorite, Spanish rice, beans, homemade tortillas and shredded steak. Coming out of the kitchen, Maria was carrying platter of hot food for her family.

"Foods done!" She yelled letting everybody know to come and eat. Leo was the first to come downstairs. He was 18 years old and Alfredo's oldest child. Amanda came in next, carrying her 8-month-old son, Abraham. Amanda was only 16 and had gotten pregnant at a young age. Her father was highly upset over his daughter's reckless sexual behavior but soon embraced being a grandfather. He loved his grandson with all of his heart. Maria's brother Oscar lived at the household. Oscar was moving to the United States next month to Odessa, Texas to work on the oil rig. His plan was to work the long hours, get paid and send his money back to his family in Tijuana. The family sat the table. Alfredo led his family in a small prayer thanking the Lord for their meal, health and wellbeing.

Alfredo had just filled his Tortilla with the thinly sliced steak, when the front door was kicked off the hinges. 4 masked men invaded their home, pointing guns. Maria dropped the plate of rice she was carrying that broke into pieces. She began to scream at the top of her lungs of the sight of the masked gunmen dressed in all black.

"Shut up!" A man yelled before he swung the butt of his AK-47, breaking her jaw.

"Please don't hurt my family. I'll give you anything you want." Alfredo pleaded looking down at his loving wife whose head and face started to swell instantly. Amanda's baby began to cry from all the loud noise. One of the intruders walked over to Amanda and attempted to grab the crying child from the safety of her mother's arms.

"Please, not my child." The gunman put the barrel to her head aggressively. The child was snatched from his mother and the business end of a Glock 357 was placed to the side of the baby's head. Alfredo, Oscar and Leo were all held at gunpoint by two of the goons. The men ordered them to lay down face first. A gun was put to Leo's head first.

BOC!

The loud gunshot sounded like thunder in the small confined space in the kitchen.

"NOOOOOO!" Alfredo yelled after witnessing his only son just get executed. Leo's brain tissues splattered on the side of his face. He could hear his daughter scream and then another loud thunderous gunshot. And then another. He knew at that moment his wife and daughter where just shot and killed. The men holding the crying baby entered the kitchen.

"Now, I have a question, Senor. I need to know who you work for and I need you to tell me the truth." The masked man said before he walked over to the stove and turned it on bake.

"What do you mean?"

"Oh so I see, even after your wife, daughter and son have just been killed, you still think this is a game." The man nodded at his henchman, who placed the barrel of his rifle to Oscar's head and pulled the trigger blowing his brains out.

"Now, how you answer will determine if I leave this child to live to be able to reproduce and continue your family's bloodline. Who do you work for, Senor?" The warm tears fell from Alfredo's cheek.

He had lost his family for working for the murderous Cartel boss, El Chico. It wasn't his choice. His alliance was forced by the Los Teccas so he obliged to their laws and politics and in the process, he had lost everything he had ever loved. In as low as a whisper, he confessed. "El Chico."

Gonzales smiled behind the black mask before he pulled a 9mm from his waistline and shot Alfredo in the head, silencing him for eternity. His life would transfer to the afterlife.

"What about the kid, boss?" One of the deadly henchman asked. Gonzales thought about it for a minute. The last time he saw Castilino, he was in distraught pain. The Los Teccas were playing for keeps. He was a loyal soldier to the Madina Cartel. This was the same cartel that provided a way for him and put food on his family's table. He was loyal to them and a product of their politics. He was a reflection of them as they were a reflection of him. A message had to be sent. Opening the oven, he laid the crying baby on one of the stove racks that instantly began to burn the baby's skin. The smell of burning flesh was unbearable. Gonzalez closed the oven door as the horrific screams of the child sounded piercing.

"Let's go." He commanded his men. The murder squad left the house in death with 6 lives being took. Castilino was willing to kill a man's entire bloodline to get his daughter back and if he didn't get her back, he was going to murder anything that had to do with Los Teccas, directly or indirectly.

S. Allen

Chapter 23

"Uhmmmm. That was so good, baby." Nicki moaned in ecstasy while she kissed Malaki from his chest to his hard rock abs. They had just finished making passionate love as the smell of fresh sex hung in the air. Malaki ran his hands through her natural curly hair as she made her way back to his lips. It had been two days since the warehouse murders, and now he was beginning to see the images of his deceased enemies. While in South Dakota, he had only shot and hit clay targets. Now that he was actually committing acts of murder, he felt like a different person. He didn't feel like himself. He was becoming a monster like his co-defendant, Poncho.

After seeing the way Poncho laid Body Bag, he knew now that Poncho was driven by a stronger force. His ambition was fueled by a different course, it wasn't revenge. Poncho killed for the love of the sport. He killed because he loved to do it. In a jungle where you had the predator and the prey, Poncho was definitely the predator. Malaki just wanted to avenge his parents' murders and after that wanted to live a normal life, without out all the guns and bloodshed.

Looking down at Nicki, his kissed her on her forehead. She looked up at him with her big brown eyes.

"Malaki, what's wrong? You have been acting differently lately. I call you and you take all day to call me back. When we do talk on the phone, you are starting to become real distant and short with me. Is it something that I did to you?"

Malaki cupped her chin softly. "No it's not that at all. I just have a lot on my mind right now."

"Well, I'm listening."

"You wouldn't understand if I told you." Malaki said debating if he could open up to Nicki. He felt he could trust her and him holding it in was mentally killing him. "As I told you, my mother and father were killed when I was a small child." Nicki nodded her head, remembering Malaki telling her about his troubled childhood.

"My father's friend took me as a child and raised me. He raised me as an assassin. He taught me the art of rifle training as well as hand to hand combat. I never played a video game, played basketball or went to an amusement park."

"Sounds like child abuse to me." Nicki responded full of concern, not liking the fact that Malaki had his childhood stripped away from him.

"You see Nicki, the reason I am here is to kill the people who are responsible for the death of my parents."

Nicki's body tensed up.

Malaki continued.

"There was a detective responsible for killing my father. I have already taken his life."

"Malaki, oh my God."

"This character Mr. Biggs is the cause for my mother being killed. I have yet to find him. Once I do, he will meet the same fate as the detective."

Nicki slowly climbed out of bed as Malaki continued to tell his deadly tale of revenge. She started to get dressed as her heart threatened to beat out of her chest. She couldn't believe that she had slept with a cold-blooded murderer. She had fallen in love with young Malaki and now her heart had been shattered by his murderous confession, her eyes began to water.

"What's wrong?" Malaki asked getting out of the bed naked, walking up behind her. He put his hands on her shoulders. She jumped from his touch. She didn't want to be touched by him. She now knew that what she thought were loving, tender, caring hands, that caressed the most private parts of the body, had been stained with blood. Grabbing her Coach bag, she made her way to the front door.

"Malaki, I have to go. I need to go and take care of something." She lied and left, leaving Malaki standing there alone and confused. He thought he was doing the right thing by opening up to her. But what he didn't know was, he just drove her away.

Once in the comfort of her BMW, the tears flowed from Nicki's eyes like the Nile River. She was crushed. Nicki really thought that she had found the man of her dreams in Malaki. He was handsome, he had his own swag that made him different and he was protective.

Not to mention, the way he stroked her pussy made her cum like no other man had made her. But to know that he was a killer drowned out all of the good in him. Nicki put her car in drive and pulled out of the hotel parking lot. Her Blackberry vibrated inside of her purse. Grabbing her cell phone, she looked at the Caller ID and saw that was Malaki and sent him to voicemail. She didn't want to see him again, let alone talk to him. It was over. She hated she had to cut him off but he had just admitted to murdering a police officer. He was high risk and she knew she had to stay on the right side of the law.

Nicki made it to her home an hour later after stopping at the liquor store to get her favorite alcoholic beverage, a bottle of Moscato Popping the top on the bottle, she took a long swig. She didn't even bother to grab a champagne glass or cup. After she punished half the bottle, she started to feel the effects of the liquor as she sat on her couch. Thoughts of Malaki began to invade her mind frame as well as her past. When Malaki talked about how his parents were killed, she empathized with him as she also had a troubled childhood. Only in her case, her parents neglected here of the tender love and care that she deserved. Instead, she was physically abused not only by her father but by her mother as well. When Nicki was only 5 years old, her father was released from Federal Prison for a bank robbery in which he only served 3 years on his sentence. Returning back to society, the world had changed swiftly in the time that he had been gone. Not wanting to risk it all again and run in a bank, he started to look for a job. Frustrated by employers not wanting to take a chance at hiring a convicted felon, he started to use drugs. Crack Cocaine was his choice. Eventually, he started to get high with Nicki's mother. Turning her out to the addictive narcotic, the two of them became crack monsters with a ferocious appetite for the drug. He sold everything in the house from the appliances to Nikki's clothes. Many days and night, Nicki would go without food and would have to sneak out of the house to the neighbors. They would feel sorry for her condition and give her a peanut butter sandwich once in a while. Nikki's childhood took a turn for the worst one night. She was sleeping when she felt something painful between her legs. It was her father's index finger exploring her innocence.

"Daddy, stop. It hurts." Nicki pleaded, not understanding why her father was doing this to her.

"Shhh. Daddy love you, okay?" Pulling her panties completely off, he began to suck on the most private part of her body. The next morning when she told her mother what her father had done, she was slapped across the face and accused of lying. The sexual abuse continued throughout most of her teenage years until her father was killed by a local drug dealer who he had owed a small debt to. Two years later, her mother died of HIV and Nicki was forced to take on the world single handedly.

Due to Nicki's childhood and what she had experienced at such a young age, when dealing with men she always seem to have trust issues. She didn't believe in giving up the goods quickly. Her love had to be earned. That's why it was hard to have a relationship because most men didn't have the patience to wait to gain her trust. But Malaki was different. How he first presented himself in the restaurant, he came across as a protector and that was something she was looking for in her life. Not to mention, she was very attracted to him. She wanted him in her life.

After finishing the bottle of Moscato, Nicki stood up from the couch and almost fell on her face. She was apparently intoxicated. Going to the table where her phone resided, she grabbed it and dialed Malaki's number. Who was she to pass judgement on anybody? Everybody had a past, and everybody lived a different life. Malaki had shown her nothing but love and respect. He wasn't just any criminal. He was seeking revenge for the death of his parents, which was considered amongst those with integrity and dignity as honorable. The phone rang 4 times before the voicemail picked up. She dialed it again only to come up with the same outcome.

"Shit!" She cursed to herself before grabbing her keys off the kitchen counter. After slipping her feet in a pair of Retro 4 Jordan's, she left out the crib in an attempt to make up and apologize to her night shining armor.

Malaki let the strong pressure of hot water relax him. He was in the shower trying to wash the sins he had committed away. He was stressed out from all the killing and now, the pain of losing the only woman he has ever loved now rested in his lap. Malaki and Poncho now knew the whereabouts Mr. Biggs has called his home. They also knew some of the most frequent spots that Killa Fred was known to visit. Poncho told Malaki that it would be in their best interest to murder Killa Fred first. Malaki didn't understand the logic. He wanted to kill Mr. Biggs and get it over with so he could return to South Dakota. Poncho explained to him that it was just that Killa Fred had to be eliminated as well. If he lived, he would be able to regroup. He had too much intel on Castilino and the Madina Cartel, and for that reason he would have to go. He didn't trust Killa Fred retaliating with a squad of lethal assassins or the Federal Government.

Malaki turned the water off and stepped out of the shower. Wrapping a towel around his waist, he made his way to the kitchen. Grabbing a bottle of water from the refrigerator, he looked on his bed at his phone and noticed he had two missed calls. Gong through the call log, he saw that the missed calls had come from Nicki. A smile came across his lips. He dialed the number and it went straight to voicemail. He tried again. Voicemail.

"Nicki, this is Malaki. Please call me back." Malaki left a message, hoping Nicki would call him back soon. Malaki then proceeded to dial another number.

"Como estas, amigo." Pancho answered.

"Poncho, when do we go and take care of the henchmen?"

"In 48 hours, my friend. We will proceed to put in the work to put Killa Fred in his resting place."

"Good. I'm ready to get this over and done with."

"Don't worry, my friend. In due time." Poncho revealed and ended the call. Malaki tossed his phone on the bed and laid back with his hands clasped behind his head. He was in deep thought. His thoughts were running a million miles per second. After he finished his business with Mr. Biggs, he was going back to South Dakota to continue his life. He was silently praying that Nicki would be at his side.

Nicki pushed her BMW down the Dan Ryan Expressway heading toward the Chicago Loop toward downtown to Malaki's Hotel. She was going to tell him that she was sorry for walking out on him and that she was sorry for passing judgement on him. She was going to express her love and loyalty to him. She was going to let him know how much she needed him in her life. Reaching in the passenger seat, Nicki grabbed her designer handbag to retrieve her cellphone.

"Damnit!" She cursed herself, realizing she had left her phone on the kitchen table.

Getting on the loop, she pushed the foreign whip at 60 miles per hour. It was way over the speed limit. Her vision was becoming blurry from the Moscato that she consumed. With her vision playing tricks on her, she didn't see the brake lights that was in front of her. When she did, it was way too late as she slammed into the back of the SUV in front of her at 60 mph. The impact of the crash threw her through the front windshield, as she didn't have on a seatbelt.

Nicki was tossed three feet from her vehicle, landing on her head. Everything to her was fuzzy. She couldn't turn her head or move any part of her body. The pain she was experiencing was unbearable as she heard the siren from the ambulance getting closer and her closer. Nicki mentally saw her and Malaki walking with her small son down a sandy beach somewhere in Orlando, Florida. The huge diamond on her left ring finger represented their commitment and love for each other for the rest of their lives. A smile came across her bloody lips at the thought of her happy ending. That was her last thoughts before she closed her eyes and escaped into the darkness of the other side.

Chapter 24

Chicago Tribune

At approximately 9:00, police responded to a horrific crime scene on the city's Westside. What has been said to be a massacre has left 7 men dead. Witness say the warehouse was used to sell and distribute heroin and was controlled by dangerous drug gang that strategically used the building for criminal activities. A witness say he was at the property to purchase drugs when two men were shot in front of him. Seconds later, another man was shot in the head. A mutual gun fight escalated to the death of four more man. The witness reported that the last men were forced at gunpoint into an SUV by a man of a Hispanic descent. Police would like anyone with information to please contact the Chicago Police Department.

Mr. Biggs tossed the newspaper on the floor. It had been two days since him and Killa Fred had heard from Body Bag. The murders had been plastered across all the local stations. They knew without a doubt that he was dead. The man who was responsible for the warehouse massacre was surely about that life. They had killed 7 men. Body Bag had underestimated his foes and paid for it. Mr. Biggs grabbed his Cuban cigar from the marble ashtray and lit the tip of it. He inhaled the sweet smoke and held it in his lungs a few seconds before he exhaled.

Killa Fred sat on the couch inside the massive office. His eyes were bloodshot red. He had treated Body Bag like a son, and he groomed him to be the thoroughbred he became. It hurt his heart to the core to know that his lil' man was somewhere getting interrogated or worse. He could be somewhere in a dark alley dead with a bullet in his head. Two 44 revolvers rested on his lap. He was ready to kill up the entire city for somebody putting hands on his family. Standing up with both pistols in his hand, he walked over to his boss's desk.

"I swear on my soul, I'm going to make those responsible for this shit to die a slow and painful death."

Mr. Biggs took a pull from the cigar. "Killa. Make no mistake about it. When we find these muthafuckas, we gone do something real vicious but until then, I want everything shut down."

"This shit is crazy. These mothefuckers know everything about us and we don't know shit about them, not even their identities." Mr. Biggs reached in his desk and pulled out a piece of paper. On it, was all the names of the men who worked for him.

'Listen, Killa and listen good. Somebody in our camp is double crossing us. Why, I don't know but this is an inside job. There is no way these bitches can have all of this info on us without somebody giving them our spots and speaking on nation business." Killa Fred tucked one of the hand cannons inside the waistline of his Ferragamo slacks as he listened intently to his boss's logic. Mr. Biggs looked over the list of names.

"We have to tie up all loose ends, Killa Fred. Take the names of this list and make them disappear. Proper, preparation, prevents, poor, performance. After these men are gone, we take the money we have and get up outta Chicago. We've milked this mothefucka for all that its worth. Let's get up outta here while we still can." Killa Fred raised his eyebrow not feeling his boss's orders.

"Wait a minute, you saying we about to run from these mothefuckers?" These niggas just killed my lil' nigga and now you scared and want to run from these pussy ass niggas. I ain't going nowhere until I find and murder they ass!" Killa Fred vowed.

"First and foremost, lower your mothafucking voice when you speak to me. Secondly, did I just here you call me scared?" Mr. Biggs got up from his desk and walked over to Killa Fred.

"Scared? Nigga, I raised your bitch ass and you got the balls to all me scared?" Killa Fred tightened his grip on the .44. Mr. Biggs noticed the veins on the back of Killa Fred hand that clutched the hammer. He smiled.

"Nigga, you don't got the heart to do it. Or do you? Go ahead, nigga! Pull that bitch. You might kill me now. But trust and believe, I'm a punish your ass in the afterlife. Better believe that."

Mr. Biggs and Killa Fred stared at each other for a minute without neither one blinking or flinching. They had grown up in the streets of Milwaukee and they were both killas and weren't afraid of death.

"Yeah, nigga that's what the fuck I thought!" Mr. Biggs said and took a seat back behind his desk

'Now, can you please hurry the fuck up and handle this shit so we can get the fuck up outta here and get to this money." Killa Fred reluctantly walked over to Mr. Biggs' desk and grabbed the list of names. After examining it, he folded the piece of paper and put it in his jacket and left the office. Mr. Biggs took another pull off his cigar. He knew that Killa Fred was in his feelings about Body Bag and he understood that. But on the battlefield, emotions had no place in war. Emotions could get you killed. Killa Fred would have to get his shit together and get back focused, and if he didnt Mr. Biggs had already made up his mind. Killa Fred would have to go. He was always taught that self-preservation was the only presentation. The enemies they had were unseen enemy. The worst kind of enemy to have. They had no clue as to who they were warring with, so it made no sense to stay a sitting duck. Once he got all his money out the streets and all his laces was tied, he was going to bounce. In his ambitious mind frame, if he could take over the Chicago drug trade he could go to any city and take over. He lost some valuable pieces on the chess board but he was still in the game. He had money, guns, and brains and that alone would get him to the top.

Killa Fred pulled the stolen Infiniti truck inside the Ford City Mall parking lot and parked next to Booveillie's cream colored Lincoln Town Car that sat high on 26 inch Forgiatos. A 38 snub nose rested under his left thigh. Killa Fred was in his body about the way Mr. Biggs had spoken to him only hours ago. He felt that Mr. Biggs had tested his gangsta and his pride was hurt.

As Killa Fred stood face to face with him, the thought of shooting Mr. Biggs at point blank range crossed his mind for the blatant disrespect. Mr. Biggs was his childhood friend and they had conquered the bloody streets of Milwaukee together. He was subordinate to his authority and leadership and for that reason, he allowed Mr. Biggs to live. He vowed that the next time Mr. Biggs talked to him with such disrespect he would not hesitate to kill him. His lil' potna was somewhere dead and his anger was about to be released on the streets.

In a way, Killa Fred was glad that he told him to single-handedly get rid of the workers that could possibly be giving information to their enemies. At this point in the game, everybody was suspect and trust was not an option. Booveillie was the first name on the list. Killa Fred had never really liked the young dope boy because he was way too flamboyant. Killa Fred had told Boovellie that he was going to front him two kilos of heroin on consignment to hustle for him on the side. Knowing he was coming to pick up some weight, he pulled up in a car with big rims instead of rolling something more discreet. Killa Fred watched as the young hustla got out of his whip, arrogant as hell.

"What's up, old school?" Boovellie greeted getting into the Infiniti truck.

"Same old shit, youngin. Trying to get to this paper. You know we gotta get it while the getting good. You feel me?"

"Ain't no secret about that." Killa Fred reached in the backseat and grabbed a Walmart shopping bag.

"Ay youngster, I wanna ask you a quick question."

"What's that?" Boovellie asked.

"You don't know nothing about the niggas that's going around killing our people, do you?"

"Hell naw, fam. You already know if I knew who them niggas was, I would've deaded them niggas myself. That's on Body Snatcher."

"Indeed. Indeed," Killa Fred replied and passed Boovellie the Walmart bag.

"Go ahead and check your product out." Killa Fred eyed the youngsta as he slid the snub nose from under his leg.

Boovellie looked in the bag, only to see some fold up bath towels. "What the fuck is this?" He turned around only to be looking down the dark barrel of small handgun.

"I believe your words to be true, youngsta. But this is much bigger than me." Killa Fred said before he pulled the trigger.

Boc!

All Boobille saw as the flash and then everything went black. His brains and pieces of his skull painted the passenger side window. Killa Fred pulled the trigger 4 more time as retribution for his lost homie. After wiping down the whip, he tossed the murder weapon in the backseat, got out of the car and jumped in Boovellie Lincoln. He pulled out of the empty mall parking lot, leaving Boovielle stinking. The Body Snatchers were taking several losses to their operation but Killa Fred was going to make sure that the streets felt his wealth.

Poncho was involved in intense game of playing Call of Duty on his PlayStation. Since coming to the United States, he had become accustomed to playing video games in his free time. Call of Duty was his favorite. It was a violent game and shooting and killing was the only way to win the game. Even though Poncho liked to play the video game, his life was very much real and the killing was his way of life. He had climbed the ranks in the Madina Cartel by spilling the blood of rival cartels in the name of this boss… Castilino Madina. Poncho was tapping on the button on the controller when his cell phone rang. Looking at the Caller ID, he answered knowing who was on the other line.

"Hola, senor."

"Poncho, I need you here immediately."

"El Jefe. Boss, we are close to getting to Mr. Biggs. We now know his whereabouts."

"Call me back on a different line. I will tell you what's going on." Castilno said before he left Poncho with the dial tone in his ear.

Poncho got up and grabbed his coat. Tucking his FNH handgun, he left out the door to walk across the street to use the pay phone. He could tell his from boss' tone that something was definitely wrong. After putting a quarter in the pay phone, he dialed the number. Castilino answered on the second ring. Poncho listened attentively as his boss brought him up to date on the move the Los Teccas had made in snatching Grace for the $100-million ransom. As Poncho listened, taking in all the information, he knew that Grace would be killed even after the ransom was paid. He knew his enemies. Poncho knew that with the Los Teccas money wasn't the issue. They could care less about the money. They controlled the pipeline to the United States. Anybody moving drugs from Mexico to the states had to come through Tijuana and would have to pay a passage fee to the Los Teccas. If the passage fee wasn't paid righteously, then the drugs wouldn't make it past the checkpoints. El Chico and the Los Teccas kidnapping Grace was a direct message to Castilino and that the message was that he could be touched.

It hurt Poncho's heart to know that after all the hard work and blood shed, he would have to abandon the struggle and abort the mission to kill Mr. Biggs. He didn't want to have to leave Malaki in the battlefield to fend for himself. He had grown to love Malaki as a brother and it would crush him if anything was to happen to his friend in his absence. But it was over his head. His boss had given him his orders and Castilino's orders were to be followed. Castilino wanted Mr. Biggs dead because he had attempted to kill him over 6,000 kilos of heroin. Castilino would piss a 6,000 keys but his daughter was in danger and her life was much more important than wasting time with a petty crook like Mr. Biggs.

Poncho walked back to his apartment. He had to go get up with Malaki and give him the news that he was on his own. Grabbing his keys, he got in his whip and was in route to go see his comrade. 30 minutes later, Poncho was pulling into the Congress Hotel downtown. He had called Malaki and told him that he was on his way and that he needed to talk to him about something important. Malaki said that he would be waiting. Getting off the elevator on Malaki's floor, Poncho walked to his door and knocked 3 times. Looking out the peephole, Malaki saw it was Poncho on the other side and opened the door.

"What's good, Eśe?" Malaki greeted in a joking manner. Poncho held a serious facial expression as he stepped into the luxurious hotel room. Malaki closed the door and locked it. At the same time, noticing Poncho's serious demeanor.

"What's wrong, Poncho?" Malaki probed.

"I have some disturbing news, my friend."

"Speak on it."

"My boss has summoned me back to Juarez. This thing with Mr. Biggs you will have to continue on your own. I'm sorry, my friend."

"What do you mean? I thought we were in this together? What about my enemies are your enemies and your enemies are my enemies?"

"Malaki, you are my friend and I have grown much love for you. You are the real deal, but I am a part of something. I must handle my staff titles and duties with the Madina Cartel. I love you as a brother, amigo but I'm subordinate to the Madina Cartel. And when they call for me, I must go. This situation with Mr. Biggs you can finish on your own. The hard part is over with. We have found where he lays his head. It took some time but we did it, brother. Now, it's up to you to squeeze the trigger and end this man's life. I trust in you, my friend. You have proven yourself to be one of the best. I know your father is looking down on you and he is proud."

Malaki listened to what Poncho said. With him or not, he was going to kill Mr. Biggs for sure. He just felt that he was losing Poncho's friendship and to him that meant more than anything. "Poncho, it's messed up that you have to leave after all that we have accomplished together but I understand. I will continue what we started and when I have Mr. Biggs head in my crosshairs, I will think about you when I squeeze the trigger." Poncho smiled at the ambition of the young man standing before him.

"I'm sure you will, Eśe but before I forget, I have something for you to help you in your endeavor. Follow me." Poncho led Malaki to the parking lot to his SUV and opened the trunk. Pulling the blanket to the side, a .50 caliber bear Sniper rifle now laid in clear view. "Can't take this on the plane with me, puta. So, I guess I will leave it here with you. I'm quite sure you can find something to do with it."

Malaki looked down at the powerful military rifle. It was the same rifle that Commander Sanchez had trained him to use. It was his favorite rifle. "Thanks, Poncho. I appreciate that. How can I repay you for your help and your loyalty?"

"My friend, you can repay me back by using it to blow Mr. Biggs' head off. Comprende?" Poncho said holding his arms out to Malaki. The two Assassin embraced in a brotherly hug.

'Oh, you can have this too, brother." Poncho grabbed the FNH handgun of his waistline and handed to Malaki. After admiring the shiny cannon that shot 5.62 armor piercing rounds, he concealed it on his waist.

"Now, my friend, it was an honor to meet you but I have to go. I have a plane to catch." Poncho gave Malaki a piece of paper with his contact number. After retrieving the 50 cal from the trunk, he passed it to Malaki, closed the trunk and hopped in the driver's seat.

"Take care, killa." He said then laughed pulling out of the parking lot, leaving Malaki holding the tool of death that would close Mr. Biggs' casket.

Chapter 25

Grace was startled when the bedroom door opened. The light from the hallway caused her to squint her eyes. All she saw was the shadow figure.

"What do you want?"

"I came to bring you something to eat." Arturo said, stepping into the room carrying a tray full of food. Walking over to the end, he placed the tray down on the edge of the bed. The smell of cheesy steak enchiladas engulfed the room. Grace looked over at the dinner tray to see the properly prepared meal. Her stomach was in her back. She felt as if she hadn't eaten in days. She grabbed the tray and savagely attacked the hot meal as if it would be her last. Watching her punish her meal without using the spoon or fork on the tray, Arturo let out a hearty laugh.

"There are utensils on the tray, you know." Grace ignored his comment and continued eating her food. Even with her mouth full and cheese dripping off of her chin, Grace was still the most beautiful woman that he had ever seen. Walking over to her, he attempted to move a strand of hair out of her face.

She slapped his hand away. "Don't touch me!" Grace screamed.

"Listen, I won't hurt you."

"Well let me go. Why are you keeping me here? Let me go home." Grace tossed the tray to the floor.

"When your father Mr. Castilino takes care of his end, we will hold up our end." Arturo said telling half the truth.

I hate you. I hate the Los Teccas and everything you stand for. My father is a very powerful man and once this is all said and done, he will get all of you involved. So, you might as well let me go."

Arturo shook his head at her stupidity but at the same time, he was turned on by her bravery as she faced her trials and tribulations. She was strong, beautiful and full of life. She had all the qualities that he was looking for in a woman. A woman to call his wife and to raise a family with. He knew that she didn't have a clue to the severity of her situation. Madina Cartel was no longer at the top of the Mexican drug trade and her current situation was living proof that Castilino's reign of supremacy was over. It was a new generation with new rules. The younger generation were much more ruthless and reckless and extreme power comes with money and murder. Politics had no room in the lucrative drug game in Mexico.

"Mamacita, you have much to learn. I give you my word, I will not let harm come to you. You are beautiful and I cannot let such beauty go to waste."

Grace was half listening to him. She noticed the silver fork lying on the floor on the side of the bed and the wheels in her head began to turn. She had to get away from the Los Teccas as soon as possible. She got up from the bed and started to pick up the mess that she had just made. Arturo watched her suspiciously. Grace saw the fork and discreetly kicked it under the bed. After cleaning up the mess, she walked over to Arturo handing him the tray.

"I'm sorry, senor, for my disrespectful behavior. It's just, I'm scared." Grace said in an angelic tone. Starring Arturo is his eyes in which she got lost in, he was handsome and his presence demanded attention. Arturo was captivated by her beauty. Taking the tray from her, he stepped closer to her as she took a step back.

"Do you mind if I shower?" She asked smelling her feminine funk from 4 days of not washing. Arturo that about it for a minute. He put the tray on the floor and pulled his .40 glock from the confines of its holster, pointing it at her. Looking into her eyes, he commanded her to strip. Grace obliged to his order and slid her dress off. Then, she unsnapped her bra, letting it fall to the floor. Arturo marveled at her flawless body. Grace crossed her arms over her bare breasts, putting her head down feeling embarrassed. Arturo broke from the trance he was in. He pointed his Glock in her direction.

"This way." He nodded toward the door.

"You try anything, I won't hesitate to shoot you. Do I make myself clear?" He threatened with finger on the trigger. Walking behind her with his weapon trained on her, he watched her ass cheeks jiggle with each step. Arturo took her to a small bathroom inside the house.

"Go ahead and shower. I will give you five minutes."

"What about soap? I need soap, dummy." Grace said with a slight attitude.

"Garcia. Vominos." Arturo yelled out. Moments later, a man came down the stairs with an AK-47 was slung over his right shoulder. Arturo whispered something in Spanish before the man scurried off. He returned shortly with a thick bath towel, a fresh bar of soap, a clean T-Shirt and a pair of Nike jogging pants. Arturo passed her the items and Grace accepted it.

"Thank you," she said flatly before she closed the door. Arturo stood posted outside the door as he heard the shower running.

Grace turned the shower on. Looking around, she saw a window above the shower. Standing on the edge of the tub, she opened the window, only to notice the window was barred in.

"Damnit." She cursed. She was being held inside of some fortress. Climbing down, she let the warm water cascade over her body. Her tears were mixing with water and going down the drain. She missed her father dearly and was really starting to wonder if she would ever see him again. She was starting to lose it. Grace knew that she had to hold it together if she ever wanted to make it out of the situation alive. Scrubbing her skin with the soap to get the dirt and grime off, she began to devise a plan. Grace knew that Arturo would be the weak link. She saw how he looked in her eyes. His lust for her would be the cause of his demise. All she had to do was play on his emotions and she would be able to escape this prison that she was in.

After taking her shower, she stepped out and dried herself off with the bath towel. Tying her long hair in a damp ponytail, she knocked on the door to let Arturo to know that she was done ready to go back to her room. Arturo opened the door and stared at the exotic figure before him. Seductively, she batted her eye at him.

"This way." Arturo stepped to the side to allow her pass. Walking in the room, Grace sat on the bed crossing her long legs.

"Do you have any lotion?"

"No lotion. I gave you the shower you asked for."

"And I said thank you. Was that not enough? Is there something else I can do to show you my appreciation?" She said stepping up to Arturo. She was so close he could feel the warmth of her breath. Arturo was shocked at the change of attitude. He was lost in her eyes until he was brought back to reality by the same man with the AK.

"Excuse me, senor. There's a call for you." He passed Arturo the cellphone.

"Speak." Arturo listened instinctively to the caller as he eyed Grace who had sat back on the bed.

"Gracias, amigo," was his only reply before he ended the call. "Your father is smarter than I gave him credit for." He said walking out the door, leaving Grace in her thoughts. He had been in a lustful bliss but now it was time to get back in his militant mind frame. Grace knew she had him right where she wanted him.

Two black SUV's pulled into the middle of a field in a small town outside of Tijuana. 4 armed men occupied each vehicle. In the first vehicle, Gonzalez sat in the passenger seat.100 million dollars sat in two briefcases in the backseat. Castilio was paying the Los Teccas the ransom in an attempt to save his daughters from his vicious enemies. Gonzales was sent to make the drop. He sat patiently waiting for his orders. A Kevlar vest covered his chest while his sweaty palms clutched a AR-15 assault weapon. 10 minutes later, a convoy of SUVs could be seen coming his way. The Los Teccas had told the Madina Cartel to not come more than 2 vehicles deep and now Gonzales had cursed his self for beign stupid. He now knew they were out manned and out gunned if the Los Teccas wanted to get on bullshit. He pulled the slide back on the rifle, chambering a round into the chamber. The vehicles stopped in front of Gonzales' truck. His phone rang. He answered the call, not bothering to glance at the caller ID.

"Step out of your vehicle with the money. Tell your men to stay in their vehicles." The caller demanded before he ended the all. Gonzales watched as the Los Teccas exited the SUV's all armed with machine guns. Black masks covered their faces as their bodies adorned military fatigues. Grabbing the suitcases from the backseat, they stepped out. Arturo opened the passenger door of one of the trucks. Walking up to Gonzales, he took a pull from his cigar.

"Drop the cases and put hands to the sky." Arturo's men surrounded the two trucks.

"I'm glad that your boss decided to follow instructions."

"Where is the girl?"

"Don't worry, my friend. She is in good hands. Trust and believe, she will not be harmed. You have my word on that." Arturo grabbed one of the suitcases, unlocked the security mechanism on it and opened it. Rows and rows of dead presidents stared him in the face. Grabbing the second briefcase, he did the same and got the same result. He handed the briefcases to one of his men.

"The girl was supposed to be here. That was the agreement. We give you the money, you give us the girl, no?" Arturo nodded to his man and at that moment, the silent desert was lined up from the sound of automatic gunfire. The Los Teccas sprayed the two SUVs down with hellacious 7.62 rounds from their AK-47s. The bullets went through the trucks like it was paper. 30 rounds magazines were emptied and reloaded and emptied again. The air was polluted with gun smoke. After the gunshots ceased, the Los Teccas went to each vehicle, opened the door and pulled the soulless corpses from the vehicles. Once the bullet riddled bodies were sprawled out on the ground, each of them were shot in the head. Gonzales knew that he would meet the same fate. He just hoped his death would be quick and painless. Arturo calmly pulled the Springfield Armory 45 ACP from his holster and placed the end of the barrel to Gonzales' forehead.

"You are an honorable soldier, my friend but there is a change in the supremacy of the Cartels. Tijauna is now at the top of the food chain. Castilino and the Madina Cartel have no place. All your politics, laws and policies have been undermined by Los Tecca. I have a message from El Chico for Castilino Medina. Whenever you see him in hell, please tell him that it is a new regime." Arturo said before he pulled the trigga on the large hand cannon.

BOOOM! The 45 jerked in his hand from the powerful recoil of the gun. Blowing Gonzalez's brains out of his hat rack, his body dropped to the ground with a loud thud. Arturo stood over his body and emptied the clip in his torso, leaving his chest full of hollow point lead. Looking around at the carnage that him and his men left, he hopped back in truck. He had come to do what he was supposed to do. To retrieve the 100 million and send Castilino's men to meet their maker. As they pulled away from the homicides they just caused, Arturo was now wondering what El Chico would tell him to do with Grace. If he made the call to execute her, then Arturo would have to make a grave decision. He would either respect his boss authority and carry out his order, or he would keep his word to Grace and buck El Chico's command. At that point, his actions would make him insubordinate. It would be something he would be able to live or die with. He would have to decide. One thing for sure, he didn't have much time to make his decision as time was not on his side.

Poncho's plane landed on a small air strip in Juarez Mexico at 6:45. It was a humid day and Poncho had a had a comfortable flight. When the plane landed, three military Hummers waited for his arrival. Stepping off the plane, he walked over to the small convoy. Men stood posted with heavy artillery. The men were part of Poncho's Federation Enforcer Group. They were trained assassins who followed Poncho's order only. The Federation Enforcer Group was a special elite team of gunmen with in the Madina Cartel. The crew of shooters were trained in accuracy shooting as well as explosives. It was the Federation Enforcer Group that caused the deaths of many of Castilino's enemies. Castilino Madina had warned Poncho to use the Federation Enforcer Group to assist him on the mission to kill Mr. Biggs, but Poncho refused. This was the time that he could exploit his own bloody talents and prove to Castilino that he was worthy of the title of being the number one killer throughout Mexico as well on the other side of the border.

The men saluted their boss. He saluted them both acknowledging their loyalty as well as subordination. The convoy traveled through the streets of Ciudad, Juarez. Poncho looked out the window as he rode through the streets that he was born and raised in, He had been gone for a year now and so much had changed since he was home. Buildings that stood before he left, were now gone. He noticed how many poor people stood in the corners. His city was for sure poverty stricken. As a young man, Poncho had a vision that one day he would help his city out financially. He had gotten caught up in killing.

An hour later, the hummers pulled into the circular driveway of Castilino's Mansion. Castilino's security awaited their arrival. Stepping out the vehicle, Poncho shook hands and saluted Castilino's personal security.

"Mr. Madina is waiting for you, senor." One of the men said taking Poncho's luggage from him.

Poncho made his way up the spiral staircase and headed to his boss's office. Poncho knocked on the door before he turned the knob entering Castilio's immaculate office. When he entered, Castilino had his back toward him obviously in a heated telephone conversation. Poncho took a seat on the couch. Castilino turned to see his trusted lieutenant. Castilino's eyes were watery and the color of fresh blood. Poncho could see the stress and frustration all over his boss' face. He could see nothing but pain, worry, and grief in Castilino's eyes.

"I don't care. I just want my daughter back. The puta, El Chico gave me his word he would release my daughter. He fucking lied!" Castilino vented into the phone. Poncho already knew that things had gotten real. And hearing Castilino, he knew that El Chico had played Castilino.

"Okay, just do what you can, please. I need my daughter back." Castilino said before throwing his iPhone against the wall, shattering it into pieces. Taking a seat at the head of his desk, he reached for the almost empty fifth of 1800 Tequila and took a swig. Since Grace's kidnapping, he had been doing nothing but drinking and smoking weed. The intoxication momentarily numbed the pain he felt for losing his only child. Poncho stood up and walked over to the desk and saluted his chief. Castilino weakly saluted him back. He was on the verge of breaking down.

"Como estas, El Jeffe." Poncho greeted his boss as well as mentor.

"They fucking lied to me. I gave them the money they asked for, Poncho. They fucking lied." The tears rolled down from Castilino's eyes and on to the oakwood desk.

"We will get her back, senor. Trust and believe." Poncho replied trying to comfort Castilino. He knew that nine times out of ten, it was a wrap for Grace, but Poncho hoped and prayed that he was wrong. If he had any chance at getting her back, he had to get actively immediately. It was only thing that Poncho could do. He had to kill off all of the Los Teccas. He was going out have to start at their chain of command and work his way up to the top. Interrogation and explicit murder would be his blueprint to get Grace back. If Grace was already dead, it was nothing that he could do. The Los Teccas hadn't confirmed her death so Poncho knew that he had a chance at getting her back. Looking into Castilino's eyes, he gave him his word that he would do all in his will to retrieve Grace, and in the midst, he would dismantle the Los Teccas for their treachery and disrespect. Not waiting for his boss to reply, he turned on his heels. No words needed to be explained. Poncho was about to turn the city of Tijuana into a pool of blood.

Chapter 26

Malaki laid in the bushes, 3 blocks away from Killa Fred's condo in a small city south of Chicago called Peoria, Illinois. He had gotten the information on Killa Fred from Body Bag the night that he was killed. He had been laying on the murderous hitter for the past 72 hours. Following Killa Fred around the city had become a hard job because he didn't have a routine. Malaki figured that this would be easier to lay and wait and then when time presented is self, he would knock Killa Fred's head from his shoulders, literally.

Killa Fred stepped out of his whip and adjusted his navy blue fedora that sat on his head. Double checking the clip to his silenced .380 seeing that it was full to capacity, he stuck the clip into the weapon and tucked the weapon in the front pocket of his coat. Calvin's name was the next on the list that Mr. Biggs had given him. It was going to hurt his heart to murk Calvin because he was from the old school and played by the rules of the game. He knew that Calvin wasn't the weak link in the chain but he had his orders, and his orders were to dead anything and everything tied to them. There was no room for favoritism, Calvin had to go. Using his gloved hand, Killa Fred buzzed Calvin's doorbell.

Calvin lived on the westside on a street called Walbash. The neighborhood was a high drug trafficking block that was controlled by the GDs. Killa Calvin supplied the GD'S with cocaine and heroin that was fronted to him by Mr. Biggs. So, it was Mr. Biggs' drugs that was sold on Walbash Street.

"It's Fred." Killa Fred answered before the buzzer was buzzed, allowing him entrance into the building. Walking into the building, Killa Fred made his way to the third floor of the apartment building and knocked on Calvin door.

"What's up, my brother. What brings you to this side of town this time of night?" Killa Calvin greeted after opening the door. Killa Fred stepped into the small apartment.

"Ain't shit, you dig. The boss just sent me over her to holler at you about something real quick." Killa Fred retorted. Calvin closed the door and locked it.

"Well, I already know what it's about, Cat Daddy. It's been a lil' slow around here lately. These niggas at war with 4 corner hustlas. A nigga got killed on this block a couple nights ago, so I told the youngstas they should close shop for a minute. The detectives been having a lot of heat over here. I wasn't able to turn in the paper for them two bricks. I got half of it right now. So, that's like a 100 geez." Calvin informed pertaining to the work he was fronted that was moving slowly. Killa Fred took a seat on Killa Calvin's couch.

"Yeah, go get that, fam" He replied. Calvin went to the back room and came back carrying a Nike duffle bag and handed it to Killa Fred. Placing the bag on the floor at his feet, he unzipped it. Inside the bag was neatly rubber band stacks of dope money. Zipping the bag back up, he leaned back on the couch. Calvin took a seat on the couch across from Killa Fred.

"Ay Calvin, you her anything else about them niggas that's been going around shooting our people?"

"Naw, brother. Just from what you told us. Other than that, I have just been waiting to hear from Body Bag." Calvin said. Hearing his comrade's name caused his chest to tighten. Killa Fred knew for a fact Calvin had nothing to do with leaking info out to their opposition but the fact was that he still had to be killed. He was going to make sure that he didn't see or feel anything. Killa Fred diverted the conversation.

"Ay Calvin, what you got in here to drink?"

"I got Grey Goose, Corona, or Kool-Aid. Pick your poison."

"Let me get a Corona, playa." Killa Fred said.

"Coming up, Cat-Daddy." Calvin walked in the kitchen. Opening the fridge, he bent down to grab a cold beer from the bottom of the refrigerator. Until he felt the steel placed at the back of his head, causing his nerves to lock up. Killa Fred stood over him with the silenced weapon at the back of his head.

"What is this all about, my brother? I can scrape up the rest of that lil' bread for you. Just give me a day or two. Killa Calvin ain't never let you down yet. Have I?" He stuttered knowing that his life was about to come to an end.

176

"This ain't bout no money, Calvin. This business here about longevity."

Pssst! Pssst! Pssst!

Killa Fred fired three rounds, splitting Calvin's cantaloupe. Grabbing the Nike duffle bag, Killa Fred left Calvin's apartment, 100 G's richer. The money gave him momentary relief from the pain and grief he was feeling for Body Bag. Killa Fred left the Westside of Chicago with another body to add to the murder rate on the battlefield of Chiraq.

An hour later, Killa Fred pulled into his driveway and parked behind his Cadillac Escalade. It was 3:30 in the morning and the neighborhood was deadly silent. The murder he had just caught had him in dangerous mind frame. Taking the key out of the ignition, he reached in the glove compartment and pushed the button to pop the trunk. Getting out, he grabbed the 100 racks, closed the trunk, and made his way toward his door.

Laying in the bushes in wait, stalking his prey like the predator that he was, Malaki focused his vision through the Night Force optic scope mounted on top of the 50 caliber Bear that sat on a tripod. The scope was equipped with an infrared heat seeking device, allowing the scope to detect a human body in complete darkness through a person's body heat. Malaki had watched Killa Fred pull into the driveway and now had him inside his scope and the cross hairs placed on Killa Fred's cranium. The silencer barrel on the rifle would make sure that Killa Fred's murder didn't wake the neighbors.

Killa Fred was at his front door attempting to put the key into the lock mechanism. Malaki focused on the shot, tightening his finger around the trigger and allowing the butt of the rifle to rest on the inside of his upper right shoulder. Taking a deep breath, he relaxed and applied a steady squeeze. The rifle jerked and released a .50 caliber projectile that found home in Killa Fred's head, practically blowing his head off his shoulders. The front of the front door was sprayed with blood, as pieces of brain meat oozed down the oakwood door.

Malaki looked back in the scope and saw Killa Fred headless body still twitching on the pavement. His life was over. Malaki unscrewed the silencer and folded the tripod on the weapon. Placing the rifle in the trunk, Malaki got in his whip and calmly pulled off. The night was far from over as well as the bloodshed. Malaki put the address in his phone into the Buick's GPS system and followed the easy directions to his next location. He was going to bust another head.

It was 5:15 am while Mr. Biggs tossed and turned in his king sized bed. He hadn't been able to have a good night's sleep since the events that were transpiring with his crew and the deadly situation at the warehouse. Not to mention, he had not heard from Killa Fred in almost two days. He knew that Killa Fred still felt some type of way about the argument they had but he knew that his man would get over it, and if he didn't, so be it. Mr. Biggs jumped out of bed hearing his car alarm going off to his S Class Mercedes Benz.

"What the fuck?" He said to himself. His mansion was located in Harvey, Illinois. His community was nothing but exclusive estates. The cheapest home on the block was priced at about 400 thousand. Mr. Biggs' lavish crib was worth 10 million in street money. His closest neighbor was at least a quarter mile away. There was no reason his car alarm should be going off. He figured it might have been some kind of animal.

Looking out of his massive window, Mr. Biggs body was now placed inside the Night Force optic scope. Malaki had a clear shot of his adversary. He laid on the rooftop of the mansion a quarter mile away from Mr. Biggs' house. The sun was about to rise so Malaki had to create a situation. He sent a silenced round from the 50 cal. The round penetrated the passenger side door of Mr. Biggs' Benz. Thus, activating the car alarm. Malaki then raised the rifle in the direction of Mr. Biggs bedroom. He had one shot, one kill. His parents' lives would now be revenged. Putting the crosshairs on Mr. Biggs face, Malaki grinded his teeth. He thought about all the years he had grown up without the opportunity to have a love in his life that only a mother could give. He thought about all the war stories Commander Sanchez had told him about his honorable father and how he would never be able to meet such a great man. The man responsible for the way his life turned out was in his scope.

Foooth.

Malaki squeezed the trigger. The round hit Mr. Biggs in the stomach, knocking out his intestine.

Foooth.

He pulled the trigger again. This time the round made contact with Mr. Biggs face, blowing his brains out through the back of his head. He was deceased before his body hit the bedroom floor. Blood thickly oozed out the large hole in his head and formed a pool of crimson red liquid that smelled of copper. Malaki laid the murder weapon down and wiped the lone tear that escaped from his eye. It was over. Mr. Biggs and Detective Calhoun were the cause of his parents' deaths and now they were traveling to the afterlife. All his countless hours of training had paid off. He had come to Chicago on a mission and that mission was complete. The murder rate in the city had reached one extensive high number of 620 homicides that year. Malaki and Poncho had contributed their fair share of bodies to the cemetery. The sun was rising. Malaki made his way off the roof and into his whip. A huge weight had been lifted off his shoulders. Now, he could live in peace and tranquility, knowing that the ones responsible for hurting his loved ones were no longer amongst the living.

Nicki was laid up in a hospital bed inside of Cook County Hospital. She had come out of her slight coma but was very much in an intensive condition. From the car crash, she suffered three broken ribs, a fractured wrist, a fractured skull and rupture spleen. Her entire body ached and the medication they were giving her did very little to numb the pain. Even in excruciating pain, her brain only allowed her mind to have thoughts of her man, Malaki. She silently prayed that he would forgive her for walking out on him when he needed her the most. Even in her predicament, she didn't care about what she was going through. She only cared about Malaki and what he was going through. Nicki prayed for his safety and wellbeing because she needed him in her life.

Malaki had continuously tried to call Nicki's cell phone, only to come up with the voicemail. He was starting to have an eerie feeling in the gut of his stomach but he could do nothing about it but hope like hell she returned his call. Malaki had two more calls to make. Dialing the number, the phone rang once before it was answered.

"Hello!" The man answered.

"It's me, papi!" The phone was silent for about five seconds.

"Malaki, my son."

"Yes, it's me."

"Malaki, if you are calling, this must mean that it is finished."

"It is finished. I have done what I was supposed to do. It took a little time but I did it!" Commander Sanchez smiled on the other side of the phone like the proud father that he was. He knew that Malaki would complete his quest for revenge. His ambition was fueled by the hate he had for the ones responsible for his parents' deaths. Commander had trained him to be lethal. His training was extreme as well as routine. He was from another breed and now that he had bodies under his belt, he was on a level rarely obtainable. He was now a thoroughbred assassin.

I'm on my way home. My business here is finished."

"I await your arrival," was all Commander Sanchez said before he ended the call. He missed his son dearly and was glad that he was coming home in one piece. Commander Sanchez knew that the streets of Chicago were nothing nice, and the gangsters that roamed in those streets played for keeps. Chicago was the murder capital of the world. Death and killing was a way of life. Most niggas in the game were in it for the money. Then, you had those that was in it for the murder. To some, killing was a fashion but to Niggas like Malaki, that murder shit pumped through his veins.

After getting off the phone with Commander Sanchez, Malaki made a phone call to Midwest Airline and booked a one-way ticket to South Dakota, his home. Malaki booked his ticket then attempted to call Nicki again. He came up with the voicemail again. He didn't want to leave Chicago without her but he had no other choice. Without Nicki, Chicago had nothing positive to offer him. He was hurt to the core that Nicki didn't return any of his calls but he had to move on with his life. Packing up his belongings, Malaki attention was caught by what was being said on the local news station. Malaki stopped what he was doing, grabbed the remote and turned the volume up.

"The body of a Chicago man was found shot to death this morning in Harvey, Illinois. The body of Larry Sullivan was found by a female acquaintance when she came to Mr. Sullivan's home after not hearing from him in a few days. Mr. Sullivan AKA Mr. Biggs is a known drug trafficker and at the time of his murder was being investigated by the FBI for charges ranging from Heroin and Cocaine distrubution as well as Murder. Mr. Biggs is the head of a Federal Indictment on the Body Snatchers, a violent drug crew controlled by Mr. Biggs and his second in command, Fredrick Dells, who was also found shot to death in front of his home only hours before Mr. Biggs was found murdered. Forensic Crime Investigators are saying the two men were killed with the same murder weapon and the recent homicides are believed to be connected. Police would like anyone with information on the violent shootings to please notify Chicago Police. Thank you."

Malaki turned off the television. It was all over now. He could now close this chapter in his life. He now knew that he could kill a man and if he had to, he would do it again. He was a bonafide shooter!

S. Allen

Chapter 27

El Chico sat in his master bedroom, sitting at his office desk that was neatly stacked with bundles of American currency, totaling 100 million dollars. It made him smile seeing 100 mill of his enemy's hard earned money. He had finessed Castelino out of the money, it was easy. Now that he had Castilino's money, he had an important decision to make. To either return Grace or execute her. This decision would pave the way for the Los Teccas. If he returned her, then it would show diplomacy as well as weakness. If he took her life, it would send a secret message to the Madina Cartel. The message was that the Los Teccas feared nothing, and the hearts of the men associated with the Los Tecca Cartel was made of stone. El Chico always lived by the knowledge and wisdom that was handed down to him from his forefathers, and that was when in a position of power, it is always best to be feared because love could easily change. Fear would remain in the hearts and minds of those that oppose you. Los Tecca's infrastructure was based on fear. El-Chico could care less about the money. He had a blood thirst for power and complete dominance. El Chico snatched his cell phone off his snakeskin belt and dialed.

"Como estas."

"What's up, Jefe Boss?" El Chico bent over the open kilo of cocaine that sat on the desk in front of him and sniffed the uncut coca. The cocaine flowed through his bloodstream.

"Kill the girl." He calmly spoke into the phone. Without waiting for a reply, he ended the call. He was going to send Castilino a present, a bag containing his only child's head.

Arturo was in a small town called Culiacan, north of Sinaloa, Mexico overseeing the mass production of methamphetamine The cartels had made billions of dollars selling cocaine and heroin in the United States, but to produce the drugs was becoming more expensive. Border patrol tightened up and beefed up the security on the checkpoints in Tijuana entering the United States. The cartels had to spend more money on securing the passage for their narcotics getting through the checkpoints. That was until the drug cartels was introduced to methamphetamine AKA.Meth. The addictive drug was much cheaper to produce, giving the Cartels more options into funneling their money into transportation fees. The laboratory Arturo was overseeing belonged to the Los Teccas and was a massive production laboratory. It only took one week to produce 243 gallons, 921 liters of liquid methamphetamine, approximately equivalent to a 1,000 pounds, 460 kilograms of solid meth, and 355 pounds. 161 kilograms of sold methamphetamine. The Los Teccas took pride in the meth that they produced and put on the streets. The exclusive ingredients they used consisted of 617 pounds, 280 kilograms of phenyl acetic acid, 15,979 pounds, 7,248kilograms of caustic soda, 2,821 pounds, 1,280 kilograms of tartaric acid; 573 pounds, 260 kilograms of sodium acetate; and 22 pounds, 10 kilograms of mercury chloride. In the final stages of production, the Los Tecca was able to produce 642 kilos of meth. This was done on a weekly basis. El Chico and the Los Teccas made millions of the chemical made drug.

Arturo walked through the laboratory carrying a Bushmaster assault rifle loaded with .223 ammunition. There was no room for error or mistakes. Millions was at stake.

While doing a round through the lab, his cell phone vibrated on his hip. Grabbing his phone, he looked at the caller ID and saw that it was El Chico calling him.

"Como estas." He answered.

"Kill the girl," was all that El Chico said and ended the call. Arturo knew that El Chico would make the decision to kill Grace. He wouldn't have it any other way. He knew that El Chico didn't have a heart, and if he did, it held no love to it. Arturo had also made a decision. He wasn't going to let anything happen to Grace. He had to get her out of the danger that she was in. Arturo didn't have a plan to say the least. He didn't even know where he would take her, but one thing he did know was that El Chico and the Los Teccas would stop at nothing until his head was off his shoulders and placed on a stick. They would put on display for the world to see what happens when you cross or betray the Los Teccas.

Arturo was a soldier, a killer and a cold-blooded shooter that feared nothing but God. It was something about Grace that made him want to take a chance and face the savage beast. He didn't know if Grace was worth putting his life on the line, but one thing for sure, he was definitely about to find out. Arturo put two fingers in his mouth and blew a coded whistle. Two minutes later, one of the workers walked up. Arturo spoke something to the man in Spanish and the man nodded his head in understanding. Arturo passed him the rifle. Making his way to his Jeep, Arturo hopped in and pulled off. He was on borrowed time. El Chico had given the order to kill and there was no telling who else had been notified about the execution. He had to get her up out of there and fast.

There were 6 armed security guards posted outside of the small house that Grace was held captive. Arturo knew that there was no way he was going to get her out of there without any blood being shed. He cursed himself for leaving the 223 at the laboratory, pulling up to the house. He knew that this was a kill or be killed situation. Parking behind a military Hummer, he took the Glock 19 out of his Velcro holster. Ejecting the standard 17 shot magazine, he replaced it with a full 30 round clip and stuck it in the butt of the gun. He pulled the slide back racking a round into the chamber and placed the glock back in its holster. It was either now or never. He stepped out of the Jeep and walked to the front of the house where the soldiers stood posted.

"Como estas." They all greeted and saluted their boss. He saluted them back and kept it moving inside the house. Walking up the stair, he went to the door Grace was being held and opened the door. Grace was in a peaceful sleep when he came into the room. She looked like a sleeping angel. He hated to have to disturb her peace but her life depended on it.

"Oye, despiertate, Grace, despiertate." He said to her in Spanish, meaning wake up. Grace woke up as he gently shook her shoulder. Grace stirred from her peaceful sleep only to see Arturo standing over her with a worried expression on his face.

"What do you want? Go away." Grace tiredly spoke.

"Get your stuff. We are leaving here at once." Grace got up and slid on her jogging pants.

"Are you taking me home to my father?" She probed.

"Just hurry up. We have to leave here." Arturo said ignoring her question. Arturo and Grace were about to head out the bedroom door when they heard footsteps rushing up the stairs. Arturo put his finger up to his lips signaling for Grace to be quiet. There was a knock at the door. Arturo opened up the door and stepped out into the hallway to see what the two men wanted, concealing the Glock 19 behind his back.

"What do you want?"

"Senor, El Chico has sent word for us to bring the prisoner to him as soon as possible."

"El Chico has not given me this message that you bring. I am second in charge and El Chico knows to respect the chain of command." Arturo retorted.

"With all due respect, we have our orders." Grace pushed her ear to the door eavesdropping on the conversation until she heard two loud rapid gunshots that caused her to jump back from the door. Seconds later, the door opened and Arturo stood before her carrying the smoking Glock.

He grabbed her hand. "Let's go." He said leading Grace out of the bedroom. Walking out, Grace couldn't help but notice the two dead bodies lay sprawled out in front of the door. Both men had been shot in the head as blood spilled from the large holes. She had to cover her mouth to stop herself from throwing up.

Descending down the staircase with his Glock extended in front of him, Arturo held Grace's hand with his other hand. She gripped his tightly while following him down the stairs. The four remaining bodyguards had heard the gunshots come from inside the home and was now checking the premise for the threat. One of the men rounded the corner only to see Arturo with his weapon trained on him. Arturo squeezed the trigger, hitting the man in his neck. The slug tore through his esophagus, like butter, killing him instantly. Arturo had to get to the safety of his vehicle. Walking past the dead soldier, Grace stopped her stride to pick up the man's AR-15. Arturo looked her as if he was thinking could he trust Grace with the AR-15. Arturo was trying to escape with the hostage. Grabbing Grace, he forced her to the ground as the barrage of bullets were sent their way. Arturo flipped the couch over, using it for cover and stuck the Glock 19 over it and squeezed. He was releasing a flurry of hell of his own. The gunman fired more rounds until his clip was empty. He ejected the magazine and was attempting to reload when Arturo leaped over the couch and rushed him, knocking him on his back. Arturo began to pistol whip the soldier. The sound of the man's skull cracking from the Glock was sickening. Arturo was in a rage until he felt cold steel being pressed against his neck.

"Drop your weapon, puta, or I blow your fucking head off." Arturo held his hands in the air, allowing the Glock to fall to the floor. He was in a no-win situation. He could almost feel the hot shell melt his brain until he heard the loud bark of a rifle. He felt something wet spray his face. Looking back, he saw the soldier grasping at his torso and then he fell forward. Arturo saw a scared Grace holding the smoking AR-15. He smiled at how this beautiful woman had just murdered another person to protect his wife. Picking up his 30 round Glock from off the ground, he motioned for Grace to follow him. She obliged. Making their way out of the house, they raced to Arturo's Jeep. He jumped in the driver's seat as she got in the passenger seat. Arturo put the key in the ignition. The engine came to life.

"Hurry, hurry, they are coming." Grace said looking back only to see two gunmen running toward the vehicle pointing assault rifles. Putting the jeep in drive, Arturo pulled out of the parking lot as bullets ping ponged off the back of the SUV, taking out the back window in the process.

"Get down!" Arturo yelled to Grace turning onto a main road. The two shooters ran to a vehicle and got in hot pursuit.

"Where are you taking me?" Grace questioned still holding the rifle and sweating profusely from all of the drama.

"I'm taking you somewhere safe."

"No, you stupid bitch. Take me home or pull this fucking Jeep over. I will shoot you. I swear I will fucking shoot you!" Grace screamed, now aiming the rifle in Arturo's direction. Arturo was about to respond until he looked in his rearview mirror and saw the black Range Rover coming up fast on them.

"Look Grace, I don't want to hurt you. I only want to help you, but right now is not the time for me to explain. It is time for shooting. You are going to have to get these fucks off our asses." Grace looked back and saw the SUV that was advancing on them quickly.

"Oh my God. What do I do?"

"Climb in the backseat. Let them get a little closer, point the rifle at the vehicle and squeeze the trigger. Simple." Arturo instructed.

The Range Rover was advancing quickly as a rifle was stuck out the window.

Cha, Cha, Cha!

The gunman hanging out of the window was firing at the flying Jeep.

"Come on, Grace. Get back there and get them off our ass." Arturo said swerving from lane to lane trying not to get shot. Grace climbed in the backseat and held the rifle up pointing it at the Range. She squeezed the trigger. The recoil of the loud rifle jerked in her hands. The bullet missed the truck completely. Aiming the rifle again, she squeezed at the front windshield. It was a good shot. The bullet pierced the windshield hitting the driver in his upper chest! Losing control of the SUV at 120 mile per hour caused the vehicle to roll over multiple times. Arturo saw the wreckage from the rearview mirror. He started pounding on the steering wheel.

"That's my mamacita!" He yelled proud of Grace for her accuracy and for saving his life for the second time that day. Grace smiled at how happy she made Arturo as she climbed back in the passenger. She had shot two people today and she didn't even know how she felt about it. One thing that she did know was the time she spent with Arturo was definitely action packed. It was way more action than she was experiencing in Castilino's mansion.

"So, I ask you again, where are you taking me?"

"Somewhere safe."

"What is your name anyway?" Grace asked. Looking at Arturo's strong facial features and shit dangerous demeanor, she was somewhat intrigued by him.

"My name is Arturo." He answered. Grace laid her head back on the headrest and closed her eyes with the rifle laid across her lap. She didn't know were Arturo was taking her but something in her heart told her to trust him. He had just rescued her from captivity and committed multiple murders to do it. Maybe, he did have her best interest at heart and he was going to get her to Castilino.

The sun was just about to set. Arturo glanced over at Grace, who was in the passenger seat asleep. He couldn't get over how Grace had saved his life. She was beautiful and full of life. He knew that El Chico and his men would stop at nothing until they found and killed him but that was something he was ready to live or die with.

Chapter 28

Poncho sat in the backseat of a military Hummer. He was a part of the hit squad that was headed to Ensenada, Mexico, a small-town north of Tijuana. Poncho had devised a plan that would bring major heat to the Los Teccas. He didn't even know where to even start looking for Grace, so Poncho figured he would put fire to the pot and start a boil. Through strategic investigation, Poncho learned that a retired DEA agent that moved to Mexico from the United States, began to work for El Chico and the Los Teccas as an operative. This man's name was Rapheal Felix. El Chico used Rapheal to investigate other cartels and their drug operation and build cases against them. It was Rapheal and his political alliances that started the snowball indictment against Cartel boss El Riqaue Sanchez, boss of the Sinaloa Cartel. Indirectly, Raphael leaked information on the Cartel, giving the United States enough ammunition to indict 56 men with time ranges from 10 years to life imprisonment. Rapheal was a major piece to El Chico and the Los Teccas. So, his life would be the trigger to draw first blood in the war Poncho was about to launch against the murderous cartel.

Looking at his watch, Poncho saw that it was 12:30 when they pulled into Ensenada. He was informed that Rapheal had a daily routine. At this time, he would be having lunch with his beautiful wife at a restaurant called the Villa. The plan was simple. They would patiently wait for Rapheal to come out of the restaurant and then snatch him up. Then, they would send a very personal message to El Chico and the man in his camp. Poncho and his team were disguised, wearing police uniforms. The men parked their vehicles on the block of the restaurant. Two at the beginning of the block, two at the end and the Humvee of Poncho's was parked directly across the street from the restaurant.

Poncho grabbed his walkie talkie and spoke into it.

"Look alive, my friends, he is coming out." Poncho said seeing Rapheal and his wife walking out the establishment. He was dressed in an all-white three-piece suit. He was carrying a brown briefcase. His wife wore a navy-blue sundress that showed off her toned legs as her hair laid down her back in a long ponytail. She was gorgeous. Poncho pulled the slide back on his 9-millimeter Barretta and placed the weapon in his side holster and exited the vehicle with two of his men in tow.

"Excuse me, can I have a word with you?" Poncho said walking up to Rapheal and his wife.

"How can I help you, officer?"

"I'm going to have to ask you to please come with us." Poncho placed his hand on the handle of the Beretta. Raphael looked at him with a confused look.

"I don't understand. What's going on?"

"Rapheal, what is this about?" His wife questioned sensing that something wasn't right.

Poncho was tired of all the extra talking and pulled his weapon from its holster. Placing it up under Rapheal's chin, he spoke. "You are coming with us. If you scream, I will shoot you. Do I make myself clear?" Rapheal nodded. At that moment, a Humvee came racing up the block and come to a screeching halt in front of Poncho. The doors flew open. Poncho grabbed Rapheal by his collar and forced him into the back of the Humvee at gunpoint. The barrel of the 9 to the back of his head. His wife began to scream until one of the men slapped her to the concrete before jumping in the Humvee with his men. Raphael's wife could do nothing but wipe the blood from her busted lip and watch the dangerous men pull off with her loving husband.

Poncho ordered his driver to drive around Ensenada. It had been an hour since they had kidnapped Rapheal, and they had been torturing him ever since. Poncho was about to lay down a crucial demonstration to let his enemies know that he was back on the land.

It had been two weeks since Malaki had stepped off the plane and put his feet back on the ground of South Dakota. While on the plane, Malaki couldn't get his mind off at Nicki. He felt that he was leaving a part of his heart. He didn't know what love felt like but he was sure it felt like how he felt about Nicki. Malaki was crushed from the feeling of not having her in his life. It was getting late as Malaki and Commander Sanchez were in the Black Hills Mountain.

They were hunting for deer. Commander Sanchez rarely went into the small town of Rapid City, only to buy propane or gas. He had built his ranch deep in the Black Hills Mountain. He lived off the land and that's how he raised Malaki. He could tell that something was on his son's mind. He had missed two shots. Something he rarely did.

"Malaki, is there something bothering you? You have been quite distant since you came back from Chicago." Commander Sanchez probed.

"When I was in Chicago, I met a girl."

"Okay. What about this girl?"

"We had an argument. She walked out and I haven't heard from her since."

Commander Sanchez smiled. He knew what his son was experiencing. Malaki was feeling the result of his first heartbreak. "If it was truly meant for you to be with this woman, then God will put her back in your life. If not, then it wasn't meant to be. Our life is already written from the beginning to the end. God has already written our script. There was no way Mr. Biggs and the detective would not meet their fate. Their death was already in waiting. Do you understand?"

Malaki nodded in understanding as he soaked up the game that his father and mentor had given. He was going to give Nicki her space. If she reached out to him, then it would be nothing for him to get back on the plane and head back to Chicago.

"Now, can you please get back focused? We don't have much time before the sun sets. I want to have dinner by 9:00."

An hour later, Malaki had shot a buck from 500 feet with a bolt action 3.08. Commander was in the back skinning the buck while Malaki strolled the internet on his iPhone. While looking at a website called Buds Gun Shop, his phone started to ring. Not recognizing the number, he reluctantly answered the call.

"Speak."

"Como estas, amigo."

Malaki smiled. "Poncho?"

"Yes, my friend. How are you?"

"I'm good, Poncho. How have you been?" Malaki asked. The phone was silent for a few seconds.

"Malaki, my friend, I am at a troubled time as of right now."

"What's wrong? What has happened?"

"Remember my boss I was telling you about?"

"Yeah. I remember, what's up?"

"Well he has enemies, very powerful enemies. They have kidnapped his only child and it is my job and duty to get her back. It is a very complex situation, my friend." Poncho said giving Malaki a brief synopsis of the drama he was involved in.

"So, why did you call me?" Malaki asked trying to get Poncho to reveal the real reason for the call.

"I called you, Malaki, because you are the only person that I trust. We have been in the battlefield together and I know that you are definitely a shooter. I need someone that I trust to assist me in getting my boss's daughter back. I need my friend."

Malaki thought about it for a minute. He could hear the desperate tone in Poncho's voice. He needed his help. If it wasn't for Poncho and his aid and assist, he would have never been able to find Detective Calhoun and Mr. Biggs. Poncho had proved himself to be a loyal friend as well as a bonafide shooter. He looked at Poncho as a real brother and he would never deny him or let nothing happen to him. Poncho was his brother in arms. "Say no more, Poncho. Can you give me a week to get my affairs together?"

"Malaki, with the men that we are dealing with, we don't have a week, my friend." Poncho and Malaki continued chopping it up with Poncho giving Malaki instruction on getting the plane ticket as well as other valuable information Malaki would need once he landed on Mexico's dirt. With Malaki on his side, the playing field had just been equaled. The terror that the two assassins would reign would be talked about for years on both sides of the border. That was for sure.

To Be Continued...
A Shooter's Ambition III
Coming soon

Submission Guideline

Submit the first three chapters of your completed manuscript to ldpsubmissions@gmail.com, subject line: Your book's title. The manuscript must be in a .doc file and sent as an attachment. Document should be in Times New Roman, double spaced and in size 12 font. Also, provide your synopsis and full contact information. If sending multiple submissions, they must each be in a separate email.

Have a story but no way to send it electronically? You can still submit to LDP/Ca$h Presents. Send in the first three chapters, written or typed, of your completed manuscript to:

LDP: Submissions Dept
Po Box 870494
Mesquite, Tx 75187

DO NOT send original manuscript. Must be a duplicate.

Provide your synopsis and a cover letter containing your full contact information.

Thanks for considering LDP and Ca$h Presents.

BOW DOWN TO MY GANGSTA

By **Ca$h**

TORN BETWEEN TWO

By **Coffee**

THE STREETS STAINED MY SOUL **II**

By **Marcellus Allen**

BLOOD OF A BOSS **VI**

SHADOWS OF THE GAME II

By **Askari**

LOYAL TO THE GAME **IV**

By **T.J. & Jelissa**

A DOPEBOY'S PRAYER **II**

By **Eddie "Wolf" Lee**

IF LOVING YOU IS WRONG... **III**

By **Jelissa**

TRUE SAVAGE **VII**

MIDNIGHT CARTEL III

DOPE BOY MAGIC III

By **Chris Green**

BLAST FOR ME **III**

A SAVAGE DOPEBOY III

CUTTHROAT MAFIA II

By **Ghost**

A HUSTLER'S DECEIT III

KILL ZONE **II**

BAE BELONGS TO ME III

By **Aryanna**

THE COST OF LOYALTY **III**

By **Kweli**

CHAINED TO THE STREETS III

By **J-Blunt**

KING OF NEW YORK V

COKE KINGS IV

BORN HEARTLESS IV

By **T.J. Edwards**

GORILLAZ IN THE BAY V

TEARS OF A GANGSTA II

De'Kari

THE STREETS ARE CALLING II

Duquie Wilson

KINGPIN KILLAZ IV

STREET KINGS III

PAID IN BLOOD III

CARTEL KILLAZ IV

DOPE GODS II

Hood Rich

SINS OF A HUSTLA II

ASAD

TRIGGADALE III

Elijah R. Freeman

KINGZ OF THE GAME V

Playa Ray

SLAUGHTER GANG IV

RUTHLESS HEART III

By **Willie Slaughter**

THE HEART OF A SAVAGE III

By **Jibril Williams**

FUK SHYT II

S. Allen

PAID IN KARMA III

By **Meesha**

I'M NOTHING WITHOUT HIS LOVE II

By Monet Dragun

CAUGHT UP IN THE LIFE II

By Robert Baptiste

NEW TO THE GAME II

By **Malik D. Rice**

Life of a Savage II

By **Romell Tukes**

Quiet Money II

By **Trai'Quan**

THE STREETS MADE ME II

By **Larry D. Wright**

Available Now

RESTRAINING ORDER **I & II**

By **CA$H & Coffee**

LOVE KNOWS NO BOUNDARIES **I II & III**

By **Coffee**

RAISED AS A GOON I, II, III & IV

BRED BY THE SLUMS I, II, III

BLAST FOR ME I & II

ROTTEN TO THE CORE I II III

A BRONX TALE I, II, III

DUFFEL BAG CARTEL I II III IV

HEARTLESS GOON I II III IV

A SAVAGE DOPEBOY I II

S. Allen

HEARTLESS GOON I II III
DRUG LORDS I II III
CUTTHROAT MAFIA
By **Ghost**
LAY IT DOWN **I & II**
LAST OF A DYING BREED
BLOOD STAINS OF A SHOTTA I & II III
By **Jamaica**
LOYAL TO THE GAME I II III
LIFE OF SIN I, II III
By **TJ & Jelissa**
BLOODY COMMAS I & II
SKI MASK CARTEL I II & III
KING OF NEW YORK I II,III IV
RISE TO POWER I II III
COKE KINGS I II III
BORN HEARTLESS I II III
By **T.J. Edwards**
IF LOVING HIM IS WRONG…I & II
LOVE ME EVEN WHEN IT HURTS I II III
By **Jelissa**
WHEN THE STREETS CLAP BACK I & II III
THE HEART OF A SAVAGE I II
By **Jibril Williams**
A DISTINGUISHED THUG STOLE MY HEART I II & III
LOVE SHOULDN'T HURT I II III IV
RENEGADE BOYS I II III IV
PAID IN KARMA I II
By **Meesha**
A GANGSTER'S CODE I &, II III

A GANGSTER'S SYN I II III

THE SAVAGE LIFE I II III

CHAINED TO THE STREETS I II

By J-Blunt

PUSH IT TO THE LIMIT

By **Bre' Hayes**

BLOOD OF A BOSS **I, II, III, IV, V**

SHADOWS OF THE GAME

By **Askari**

THE STREETS BLEED MURDER **I, II & III**

THE HEART OF A GANGSTA I II& III

By **Jerry Jackson**

CUM FOR ME I II III IV V

An **LDP Erotica Collaboration**

BRIDE OF A HUSTLA **I II & II**

THE FETTI GIRLS **I, II& III**

CORRUPTED BY A GANGSTA I, II III, IV

BLINDED BY HIS LOVE

THE PRICE YOU PAY FOR LOVE

DOPE GIRL MAGIC

By **Destiny Skai**

WHEN A GOOD GIRL GOES BAD

By **Adrienne**

THE COST OF LOYALTY I II

By Kweli

A GANGSTER'S REVENGE **I II III & IV**

THE BOSS MAN'S DAUGHTERS I II III IV V

A SAVAGE LOVE **I & II**

BAE BELONGS TO ME I II

A HUSTLER'S DECEIT I, II, III

S. Allen

WHAT BAD BITCHES DO I, II, III
SOUL OF A MONSTER I II III
KILL ZONE
By **Aryanna**
A KINGPIN'S AMBITON
A KINGPIN'S AMBITION **II**
I MURDER FOR THE DOUGH
By **Ambitious**
TRUE SAVAGE I II III IV V VI
DOPE BOY MAGIC I, II
MIDNIGHT CARTEL I II
By **Chris Green**
A DOPEBOY'S PRAYER
By **Eddie "Wolf" Lee**
THE KING CARTEL **I, II & III**
By **Frank Gresham**
THESE NIGGAS AIN'T LOYAL **I, II & III**
By **Nikki Tee**
GANGSTA SHYT **I II &III**
By **CATO**
THE ULTIMATE BETRAYAL
By **Phoenix**
BOSS'N UP **I , II & III**
By **Royal Nicole**
I LOVE YOU TO DEATH
By Destiny J
I RIDE FOR MY HITTA
I STILL RIDE FOR MY HITTA
By **Misty Holt**
LOVE & CHASIN' PAPER

By **Qay Crockett**

TO DIE IN VAIN

SINS OF A HUSTLA

By **ASAD**

BROOKLYN HUSTLAZ

By **Boogsy Morina**

BROOKLYN ON LOCK I & II

By **Sonovia**

GANGSTA CITY

By **Teddy Duke**

A DRUG KING AND HIS DIAMOND I & II III

A DOPEMAN'S RICHES

HER MAN, MINE'S TOO I, II

CASH MONEY HO'S

By Nicole Goosby

TRAPHOUSE KING **I II & III**

KINGPIN KILLAZ I II III

STREET KINGS I II

PAID IN BLOOD **I II**

CARTEL KILLAZ I II III

DOPE GODS

By **Hood Rich**

LIPSTICK KILLAH **I, II, III**

CRIME OF PASSION I II & III

By **Mimi**

STEADY MOBBN' **I, II, III**

THE STREETS STAINED MY SOUL

By **Marcellus Allen**

WHO SHOT YA **I, II, III**

SON OF A DOPE FIEND

S. Allen

Renta
GORILLAZ IN THE BAY **I II III IV**
TEARS OF A GANGSTA
DE'KARI
TRIGGADALE I II
Elijah R. Freeman
GOD BLESS THE TRAPPERS I, II, III
THESE SCANDALOUS STREETS I, II, III
FEAR MY GANGSTA I, II, III
THESE STREETS DON'T LOVE NOBODY I, II
BURY ME A G I, II, III, IV, V
A GANGSTA'S EMPIRE I, II, III, IV
THE DOPEMAN'S BODYGAURD
Tranay Adams
THE STREETS ARE CALLING
Duquie Wilson
MARRIED TO A BOSS… I II III
By Destiny Skai & Chris Green
KINGZ OF THE GAME I II III IV
Playa Ray
SLAUGHTER GANG I II III
RUTHLESS HEART I II
By Willie Slaughter
FUK SHYT
By Blakk Diamond
DON'T F#CK WITH MY HEART I II
By Linnea
ADDICTED TO THE DRAMA I II III
By Jamila
YAYO I II

A SHOOTER'S AMBITION I II

By S. Allen

TRAP GOD

By Troublesome

FOREVER GANGSTA

GLOCKS ON SATIN SHEETS

By Adrian Dulan

TOE TAGZ I II

By Ah'Million

KINGPIN DREAMS

By Paper Boi Rari

CONFESSIONS OF A GANGSTA

By Nicholas Lock

I'M NOTHING WITHOUT HIS LOVE

By Monet Dragun

CAUGHT UP IN THE LIFE

By Robert Baptiste

NEW TO THE GAME

By **Malik D. Rice**

Life of a Savage

By **Romell Tukes**

LOYALTY AIN'T PROMISED

By Keith Williams

Quiet Money

By **Trai'Quan**

THE STREETS MADE ME

By **Larry D. Wright**

BOOKS BY LDP'S CEO, CA$H

TRUST IN NO MAN

TRUST IN NO MAN 2

TRUST IN NO MAN 3

BONDED BY BLOOD

SHORTY GOT A THUG

THUGS CRY

THUGS CRY 2

THUGS CRY 3

TRUST NO BITCH

TRUST NO BITCH 2

TRUST NO BITCH 3

TIL MY CASKET DROPS

RESTRAINING ORDER

RESTRAINING ORDER 2

IN LOVE WITH A CONVICT

Coming Soon

BONDED BY BLOOD 2

BOW DOWN TO MY GANGSTA

A Shooter's Ambition 2

www.ingramcontent.com/pod-product-compliance
Lightning Source LLC
Chambersburg PA
CBHW070502260626
47161CB00004B/1425